£ 4

D0634996

THE LIGHT FANTASTIC

RHONA RAUSZER

The Light Fantastic:
Skye Folk and Fantasies

edited by Linda Williamson

Polygon

First published in Great Britain in 2005 by
Polygon, an imprint of Birlinn Ltd
West Newington House
10 Newington Road
Edinburgh
EH9 1QS

www.birlinn.co.uk

ISBN 10: 1 904598 35 8
ISBN 13: 9 781904 59835 0

The publishers acknowledge subsidy from the

Scottish
Arts Council

towards the publication of this volume.

British Library Cataloguing-in-Publication Data
A catalogue record for this book is available
on request from the British Library

Typeset by Hewer Text (UK) Ltd, Edinburgh
Printed and bound by Thomson Litho, East Kilbride

To my mother Mairianna
and her mother Rebecca

Contents

Editor's Note

The Light Fantastic: Skye Folk and Fantasies is Rhona Rauszer's second volume of short stories. The first collection, *Consider an Island: An t-Eilean Sgitheanach* (Polygon, 2004) featured the author's BBC Radio Scotland broadcasts from the 1960s and 1970s. The present work has a wider scope with orally composed, new stories, and previously unpublished writing.

'Pidgeon's Eggs' was Rhona's first story, written in the early 1940s. The delusions of an innocent artist, captivated by a Catholic culture and brought home to reality by an intelligent Scottish sleuth, were to become typical themes in the Rauszer corpus (see 'All on a Summer's Day' and 'Spitting Image'). Full of fun and mischief, cheek and wit are 'Hairy Lady', 'The Lonely Loch', 'Skye Fever' and 'Aurora, the Goddess of Dawn'. There is a wild strain of excitement and frenzy in the two monologues 'Nothing Leads to Nowhere' and 'Old New Year's Day', one of several genuine accounts in this work. With her husband, Kazik, Rhona recreates a zany motor trip taken together in 'Riley the Poltergeist'. From this period are seven stories recorded and broadcast by BBC Radio Scotland, in 1966 and 1968: 'Seeing is Believing', 'The Changeling', 'The Face in the Pool', 'Golden-haired Maiden', 'The Lonely Loch', 'Tinker's Tale' and 'Camisutory'. Her most recent compositions, recorded orally for publication in the summer of 2004, are 'The Silo', 'Isle of Wings', 'The Druid Tree' and 'Stem of Infinity'. 'Spitting Image' is Rhona's longest and most dramatic tale, begun as an oral narrative in the 1990s and completed during the summer of 2003. The short piece opening the collection, 'An Sìthean', was taken from diary extracts of the 1980s.

The thirty-one stories fell naturally into three groups, echoing the author's life cycle on and off the island. The first set of eleven (Skye Folk) are based in south Skye, home of ancestral clans; the following seven stories (Fantasies Apart) tell of experiences and encounters away from the island, and the last group of thirteen (Northern Lights) returns to the northern peninsula of the misty isle. The final story, 'Stem of Infinity', with a walk into the Cuillins, is the author's latest work, recounting a traditional Highland death.

A visit to the Quiraing (the Isle of Skye's mighty volcanic ridge, sixty million years old), the River Rha, the villages of Staffin and Uig in Trotternish; or a tour round spectacular roots of volcanoes making up the Red Cuillins towering over the villages of Broadford and Breakish in south Skye would give the reader an exhilarating backdrop for Rhona Rauszer's stories. The most truthful context, however, will be found in the author's autobiography, *Ultima Thule: The Life of an Island Daughter*, published together with this work.

The factual basis to many of Rhona Rauszer's stories is illustrated in the powerful setting of 'Spitting Image', when the young Effie Mathieson takes up employment with Professor Arkley in Glen Conon. Effie recalls a story of the river flooding a graveyard, leaving coffins and skeletons upturned in its wake. Historical sources tell of the Uig Estate owner's eviction of tenants in the 1870s; then a massive flood of 1877, when the River Conon loosened graves around the manse of the Estate leaving behind bodies in the laird's dining room.

Mrs Rauszer's island English is grounded in the Scottish Gaelic, the language of her Skye forbears. Colloquial phrases are always retained, following the author's indigenous island grammar and word choice. Vernacular Gaelic arises naturally in storytelling and is translated nearly always on the spot for listeners (recalling that the scripts were originally written for broadcast to an audience of non-Gaelic speakers). The meanings of phrases or words not shown on the page are provided in the Glossary. In a few stories, for example, 'Pipe Dreams' and 'Riley the Poltergeist', phonetic spellings of mispronounced English are used in dialogues to vivify the characters. For Gaelic words and phrases, the basic Guide to Pronunciation should prove useful to non-speakers.

I should like to acknowledge the linguistic assistance of Neil Macgregor, my Gaelic tutor, and the aid of my landlord David Campbell, without whose endless support and encouragement I should never have managed the three books.

Linda Williamson
Edinburgh 2005

Skye Folk

An Sìthean

The Skye MacKinnons based in Strath from the beginning of time were (according to my grandmother) fairies, sìthean, small people, peaceful and talented. They often lived in caves; some of these caves are along the Kylerhea road and some on the way to Torrin. The fairy folk in Breakish and Kylerhea hid in caves (some say they were Fionn warriors). But my grandmother said they were very small – the men bandy and hairy, the women attractive and very creative. They chose to live underground because of the giants from Glenelg, who would invade across the narrows* and finally slaughtered many of them.

My grandmother was a MacKinnon before she married her cousin Angus MacLeod. Many MacKinnons have a crooked pinky (congenital arthritis, no doubt – their caves were damp). They also have the second sight; I myself frequently foretell events before they happen.

Once, walking from Broadford to Kylerhea on a hot summer's day (about nine miles) I sat on the narrow bridge at Sgùrr na Coinnich,† the steep hill heading down to the valley below, and towards the ferry on my right, Beinn Aslaig. Spelt another way (còinneach) it could mean a mossy ben; but for my grandmother, Beinn Aslaig meant the Mount of Dreams. Looking across at it I became limp and stretched

---

* the narrows – the straits of Kylerhea
† Sgùrr na Coinnich – Height of the Meeting, the twin peaks of Beinn na Caillich and Beinn Aslaig

out on the bridge, gradually falling sound asleep. Had I moved one inch to my right I would have fallen down to my certain death.

Instead, I dreamed that a huge hole opened on the safe side of the bridge and fortunately I leaned that way towards it, because there were people inside. They seemed to be beckoning to me urgently; they were all people I knew and seemed to be at a wedding, the wedding of Alasdair MacKinnon, a handsome young doctor from Broadford. I made a move to join them and in so doing woke up to find myself safely in the middle of the road. I dread to think what would have happened if I had turned the other way – and the strange thing is – about a month later I received an invitation to Alasdair's wedding in London to Ramsay MacDonald's daughter. That's how long ago it all was.

One time I stood and watched a fat-bellied bird perched on a naked branch, and all the trees and ferns and fences were dripping in a warm mist, a Skye mist, for this was October in the Isle of Mist. A time when the phantoms leave the mountains and the graves and seek the company of man. But maybe you're not the sort that believes in spooks, sìthean or second sight. And you'd be wise not to, 'For no good can come of it,' my grandmother would say, adding in her native Gaelic, 'Ma chreideas thusa ann a'gheis bithidh a'gheis a'cumail ort' (meaning, if you believe in superstition, superstition will dog you). And in my case she was right. I have never been able to cut my nails on Friday or bring hawthorn blossom indoors, or burn less than two candles on a dinner table. Or wash my hands in the same bowl of water as anyone else without making the sign of the cross on the surface.

Once sitting cross-legged on the Fairy Bridge by Dunvegan, I was given this verse:

An Sìthean

Not warlocks or witches or goblins or spooks
Would my own father's son now decry,
For on medallion's stone bridge
Sat the last of the witches of Skye.

Isle of Wings

The old manse, derelict yet still inhabited, was up high on the hill and surrounded by sinister-looking trees; they, too, were inhabited – by pigeons, coorie doos that kept cackling-cackling all through the early hours of the morning. Frances lay in this darkened room with heavy velvet curtains and a cheep of light coming through the window. The snow was still falling outside but gradually thawing; she could hear the nearby river in full spate tumbling down the rocky hillside, captured at a certain point by the otters who were making a reservoir for themselves – gathering rotten wood, rubbish, parts of derelict fence stubs, anything they could find to prevent the river continuing – so that they could catch some of the fish coming downstream or going upstream, as the case might be. She sometimes thought she could hear them playing and splashing in the water. But that was her imagination again.

Her imagination was very vivid. She was very sad having to live here in this isolated spot with an ancient, half blind aunt since she herself was virtually an orphan. Her mother and father had died of tuberculosis. She had been sent in the Royal Mail coach, which made its way between Dunvegan in the north end of Skye to Glasgow and back, put aboard this vehicle and brought to stay with her aunt. It was a very, very different lifestyle she would have to lead. Her mother and father had been gay and happy, bright, outgoing people; whereas her aunt was a wizened, withered old stick who'd lost her minister husband and was relying entirely on her religion which came out of her in doses morning, noon and night. She saw to it that her niece would be equally conversant with the *Holy Bible* and all the religious books she had accumulated on her sloping shelves smothered in dust and cobwebs as they were.

But Frances had found one book that fascinated her more than any of the others. She had been used to reading stories about Pollyanna when she was at home with her mother and father. But now it was just the *Holy Bible* or *Dante's Visions of Hell*. This volume that her aunt had of the Visions was illustrated, and Frances was fascinated with them. She would sit up in bed at night, her candle lit and burning on the side table, this great big volume balanced on her knees. There were pictures of bodies, tiny little naked bodies clambering up sheer rocks, trying to escape from the huge flames coming out of a sort of basin that was the centre of the earth. They were in her imagination screaming and yelling in total desperation. And the tears would flow down her cheeks as she thought of the horror, what could happen to her if she should be a bad girl or do anything wicked in her lifetime.

She was only seven when she came to live with her aunt, and she tried her very best to be good, to be helpful. She did most of the work as her poor aunt could hardly see anything. All the washing had to be done in the scullery; the great big cauldron had to be boiled up, the clothes taken out of the steaming water with a stick, then rinsed off again in the sink and carried out to the washing line. All these jobs Frances did for her aunt. Sometimes she enjoyed it even: on a windy day taking the huge linen sheets out, hanging them on a rope that ran between the trees and a washing post. The wind would inflate the sheets and make her think of sailing ships. Then they would deflate and inflate again, all very exciting if there was a really strong breeze.

Sometimes when she hitched the end of her washing line to a huge pine tree or a sinister yew she would think of the nearby graveyard, and how the roots of all these trees must make their way underground to the graveyard. One of these days she wouldn't be surprised at all if the roots got under the coffins, and pushed them up, threw the bodies out into the open air. What a sight that would be! Something like *Dante's Visions of Hell*.

She was a fanciful lass and there's no doubt about it. That's why her mother had called her Frances, 'Fran' for short. Like St Francis of Assisi she would talk to the birds and chat with the trees, cuddle the rabbits and seem to have a love for all things in nature. But she had no great love for her aunt. Now she felt she must go indoors and start to make the porridge. But before that, she had yet one other item to hang on the line: her aunt's bloomers, knee-length knickers split down the middle 'for convenience sake' her aunt had said. It was a custom in those far off days for women to wear such underwear.

Re-entering the manse kitchen Fran put the porridge pot on the enormous range that stretched from one end of the wall to the other. It heated all the hot water too, was a really fine piece of engineering. The enormous water tank filled a corner of the room. The washings were sometimes taken outside in a big wooden tub, and then they would use a dolly peg to stamp the clothes; a sweet looking thing Fran thought, it reminded her of a little girl or a doll. About three feet tall, a wooden post with a wooden skirt round it and three or four legs, you had to pummel this thing up and down on the clothes that were in the tub. A scrubbing board was used as well of course and plenty of carbolic soap.

Fran stirred the porridge with a wooden stick and dished it out in little round bowls which were very pretty with flowers on the sides, very beautifully decorated; as indeed were the chamber pots underneath every bed in the manse. Some of them had poppies on the side and some forget-me-nots, all beautifully decorated. In fact, her aunt had had some very fine things. In those far-gone days the ships used to come in to every quayside, every port round the islands, particularly in Skye; there would be ships galore in Broadford, in Kyle, in Portree and up the north end. Some smaller ships would be in Lochnabéist that lay some five miles further away from where the manse had been built; so called because at one time the loch had been visited by some great monster. There used to be houses; in fact, Lochnabéist was the village of Kyleakin before Kyleakin was built. And some say that this great beast was in fact the Loch Ness Monster, which had travelled up there for its summer holidays.

Breakfast was never eaten until The Book had been read. Fran would sit on a little wooden milking stool and during the prayer she would have to turn round, arse for elbow as they say, backside foremost I would prefer, kneeling with her eyes shut and her little hands clutched together. During the reading her aunt had to have a lit candle because she was very blind now. So Fran placed the candle on the American cloth that covered the pinewood table in the centre of the room.

Many things brought by the ships were of American origin, and nearly every house had bought something or other from the sailors. Her aunt had an ebonised clock with a brass face that was, I suppose, hand-carved and very elegant. There were also brass spittoons on either side of the fire. (I think they were called in those days, cuspidors.) Every house had antimacassars on the chairs. Fran thought them hideous: some had pictures of camels and Arabs in long dresses, the colours loud and garish, she never liked them. Even the churns for making the butter had come from other countries; her aunt's had come from

Norway, a three-legged affair that stood outside in the garden. There were numerous things brought over from every country, Russia, Norway, Sweden, Denmark, you name it. Sometimes Polish men would come and knock at the door selling ocelot and other skins that had fantastic names Fran had never heard of before. But her aunt would buy pieces from them. With a huge darning needle and an elaborate silver thimble Fran was taught how to make slippers out of these bits of fur. It was so sore pushing the great long darning needle through the leather that her little fingers would be bleeding by the time she got anywhere near finishing a pair. Then, after spending about four years with this eccentric aunt, Fran was now aged eleven, disaster – catastrophe hit the manse.

Fran had gone outside to the scullery, a sort of shed. There she would get hold of a beautiful big clam-shell, shaped like a fan. This was used to lift the thick cream off the top of the basins that were setting. They were flat, round, large basins and plenty of cream could be scooped off the top of each; there were about five basins in a row. The cat of course would get some of the whey that was underneath and Fran had already set the breakfast table up with the candle lit and The Book at its side, the porridge bowls all ready. So they would have their porridge and cream after the reading was done.

She saw Duncan the Post clambering up the hill pushing his bicycle and ran to meet him. She didn't think there would be much post for them, certainly none for her. Then, she heard horrific screams coming from the house. Even Duncan could hear them, so he threw down his bicycle and rushed up to the house. Fran and Duncan managed to get in. There was smoke billowing from everywhere and the old woman was crying and screaming; Duncan got a hold of her and dragged her outside, rolled her about in the snow. Fran shook her shawl and replaced it round her. There was nothing much they could do about the house. It was all aflame. Fran worried about her little teddy bear that was on the stool where she'd left it. And she wasn't too sure whether the cat was in or out. But she got down on her hands and knees, crawled into the kitchen and found the little teddy bear with its green jumper and its amber yellow eyes. She couldn't live without it. She noticed that everything was ablaze, even the ornamental clock – evidently, the old girl must have accidentally pushed over the candle, and it had caught onto the American cloth, very susceptible to burning.

In no time at all there was a lot of shouting outside and people were rushing up, men, and women; crofter wives had taken their half bottle of brandy out of the back of their wardrobe cupboards and generously brought it with them, to comfort her poor old aunt. They soon looked after her, insisted, and indeed quarrelled about who should take her and to which croft house. She had quite a few friends amongst them, she would be all right and well cared for. Fran mingled with the children who had all come galloping up screaming, shouting and terribly excited, but very useful. They got buckets and went to the river, hauled up water bucket load after bucket load. Some of them tried to get into the house after loot. But Fran knew that somehow or other she would have to escape the grown-ups' attention – they hadn't noticed her so far – they would undoubtedly put the blame on her. They didn't know her, she'd met very few of them, she didn't even go to school. She'd been taught by her father before she came to live with her aunt, and her aunt didn't seem to think she needed any further education.

So poor Fran hid for a while in one of the outhouses while she tried to think what on earth she could do to find a home for herself. And then she thought . . . thought about the tinkers. They were around at this time of year. They always got handouts round about the New Year. She knew one or two of them quite well and indeed she liked them very much. So she started off, trying to find where one of them camped out in a cave along the coast – but Fran didn't think she'd be there at this time of the year, the woman would be more likely to be hiding in one of the empty croft houses that were derelict here and there.

So Fran began to walk and walk, it was late in the day, the winter darkness was coming down and the clouds were now racing each other to hide behind the big thick clouds of night. They looked like white angels scurrying with their wings fluttering as they raced over the night sky. And Fran thought, 'Well, that's why Skye was called Eilean Sgitheanach, the Isle of Wings,' because indeed those clouds looked very much like angels' wings to her.

Musing as she was, sitting on a rock surrounded by snow, quite thick snow now, she suddenly felt the presence of someone behind her; and turning round she saw Màiri Bhàn, one of the tinkers. She was too crippled to follow the rest of the travelling folk as they went on their way, and she must be living rough somewhere. So, Fran confided in her. She was a fine-looking woman; they called her Màiri Bhàn, because in her younger days she had beautiful, gold blonde hair with a huge bun at the back of her neck. She always wore very long dresses and before she had fallen and crippled herself she used to be a very elegant walker, striding along like an Indian princess. But now she was old and bent and haggard, but kind as ever.

'Come with me, a ghaoil,' she said in the Gaelic (come with me, my love). Fran eagerly placed her small frozen hand in the large, warm life-giving palm of Màiri Bhàn. Suddenly there was the sound of a distant stag bellowing in the woods. Fran was shivering with fright and cold, so she tightened her grip of Màiri Bhàn's hand and felt reassured.

She had no alternative now. She couldn't do anything else, she had to trust in Màiri Bhàn, and Màiri Bhàn knew the territory round about here like the back of her hand. She knew all sorts of shortcuts through the terrain, secret passages. She found her way from the Kyleakin district to Rudha na Caillich and round by the edge of the sea till they almost reached Kylerhea. Then she took her cross country to the foot of Beinn Aslaig where her secret cave was: a long deep tunnel at the foot of the mountain, well hidden by all kinds of growth, high trees, short trees, burnt-out bracken and old heather clumps, you name it, it was well hidden anyway. But eventually they got to it, and there were still the embers of a peat and wood fire at the mouth of the cave.

It didn't take Màiri Bhàn long to rouse it up again, she replenished the fire with more dry wood she brought out of the cave. It was a fascinating old fireplace, a magic circle of stones of different sizes, some flat, some round, some pointed. And they were all still warm, so they were able to sit and put their hands on them, and put their clothes on them even. It had stopped snowing now, there was a breeze and they were getting almost dry. So Màiri Bhàn took her into the cave. She was fascinated to see bundles of hay all round the edge of the cave and plenty of fish-boxes to act as chairs and tables. Fran began to feel happy again, although she was very worried about her aunt.

'Oh never mind that old faggot!' Màiri Bhàn would say. And she looked in a box of Carr's biscuits, an ancient tin box; there were pieces of bread, pieces of cheese, crowdie and some bits of chicken. So they had a bit of a feast. They even had some milk.

Fran said, 'How did you get the milk?'

And Màiri Bhàn said, 'Well, some of the cows of course. I went out late after the proper milking was done, drained off anything that was left in the teats of the cows, that's how I got my milk.' So they snuggled up together, wrapped in old blankets and confided in each other.

Màiri Bhàn told of how her man, John, had been drowned in front of her very eyes: 'He'd gone to get some lobsters out of some creels he knew about down there in the straits of Kylerhea. Well, everyone knows those straits are very dangerous waters. When a storm gets up there are vortexes that are terrifying, just as bad as the vortex in Corrievreckan. And most wise men avoid going near the water when it's so disturbed. But John was determined to get himself a lobster or two, and, as he knew there was an old boat pulled up at the side of the loch, he pushed it out. It had a mast. But he didn't check to see if it was sound, and it was a very old boat, rotting and he took a great risk with it. However, he got it out into the middle of the stream, the wind got stronger and the vortexes began to churn up, even the seagulls were giving him a warning. They came flying down towards him, their wings and their wee legs spread out, to resist being dragged into the terrifying vortexes.

'But all this was too much for my John, and so he clung on to the mast and did everything he could. The whole thing capsized on to its side and John clung on as long as he could. All you could hear him shouting was, "Màiri Bhàn! Màiri Bhàn!" and then in Gaelic, "Mo ghaol ort fhéin a Mhàiri Bhàin, beannachd leat a Mhàiri Bhàin!" (my love on you, blonde Mary, good-bye blonde Mary). Gradually he sank, and the boat was seen no more. Some men found him next day and hauled him ashore. Then it was that your uncle, the minister, who knew John very well, because the minister had the habit of having one or two over the eight when he went to meetings – he wasn't very careful with the drinking. And one night after he was at a meeting in Kyle, coming home had mounted his horse, was galloping on his way back to the manse when he fell off into the ditch and hurt his leg badly and his head. And his hat was squashed like a pancake. He was as drunk as a coot . . . and it was my John that found him in the ditch, got him remounted on his horse, brought him home to the manse and never said a word about the drinking to any living soul. So your aunt was very grateful about that, and so was the minister.

'Poor John, instead of being buried in an unknown grave, as we do with our folk, was buried in the churchyard; although he didn't have his name about the grave, he was in sanctified ground. And I was happy about that. I think of him often . . . the day we were married gypsy style – both of us peeing into the same chamber pot and exchanging blood from our wrists – those were the days!'

Fran was getting sleepy now, but she thought she'd better exchange a story of some sort. So she told Màiri Bhàn about when she was a little girl staying with her aunt, when she first came up here to Eilean Sgitheanach. She was playing outside, she was very young, when she found a bird's nest in the dyke . . .

'There were about six little chicks in it and they seemed to have no mother and nobody looking after them, they were all squawking and squawking. I thought they must be very cold and very hungry, this was no place for them to be. So I picked them all up, put them in my pinny, and went back to the house. My aunt was not in at the time, so I laid them down on my aunt's chair and proceeded to empty the kitchen dresser drawer, one of them. I cleared it all and then went outside, got some hay, lined it with hay, made it look like a nest and put the six little chicks in the drawer. Then I shut the drawer leaving just enough space for them to get air, and went outside with a fork to dig up some worms for them to eat.

'But when I came back in, my aunt had already returned and was looking all over the place with a poker in her hand for mice saying, "There must be some mice, there must be. There's mice, I can hear squeaking and squeaking!" I didn't dare open my mouth or say a word. Then my aunt discovered at long last that they were inside the drawer, she was furious. She said, "We can't have this, we just cannot have this! You must take them back to where you found them, they can't live in a drawer."

'Well, I couldn't understand why not, but I obeyed my aunt and reluctantly took the wee birds back, put them in the nest I'd taken them from. But there's no doubt, the mother would never come back to them and I think through time they would perish.'

Those few days with Màiri Bhàn were the happiest in young Fran's life. They spent their time repairing pails and buckets and pots. Màiri Bhàn was after all a tinker, and a very professional one at that! She was very good at mending anything that was made from tin. She also wove baskets and had many other skills, knew all about the herbs and puinneags and edible things round about. She even managed to grow some cos lettuce that she ate with sugar. Sometimes Fran would help her to put up the tent, a wonderful tent made of bent willow wood, covered in all kinds of things, fascinating: raincoats without buttons, pieces of sail cloth, old bedspreads, you name it! It was quite a picture to look at. And inside was warm and cosy, used mainly as a dressing room, and there was a lavatory. Then they would go for long walks across and down the valley, a very, very deep and steep one at the foot of Beinn Aslaig. Its name means the Mount of Dreams and you could dream a lot when you looked out across the frozen snow, all glittering in the morning sunshine like diamonds.

Then they would go right down to the base of the valley and Màiri Bhàn would tell her, 'Once upon a time hundreds and thousands of years ago the sea had reached right up. Sometimes in the little riverlets, you could find seawater whelks, in fresh water streams: this was proof that the sea came all this way up many years ago.'

One day Màiri Bhàn decided to take Fran down to the village again, so that she could make contact with other children. It was getting close to Hallowe'en and Fran could join the children, they would go all around the crofts and houses, sing the traditional song,

> Get up good wife and shake your feathers,
> Do not think that we are beggars
> Hog-a-ma-nay, Hog-a-ma-nay
> Give us a penny and let us away!

And sure enough, the folk in the houses would give them all kinds of good things, bits of clootie dumpling*, some milk maybe, sweeties, oatcakes. There was one house where the lady was particularly good to the children, she was good to everybody really. She was a Welsh woman, a retired opera singer, a real lady; her name was Gladys Featherstone. She would have the children in and would put chestnuts in the fire – if they clung together you would know the name of who would be your future husband. All kinds of jokes she played with the children, she taught them to sing little songs. Indeed she was a remarkable woman herself, had been the Madame Butterfly of her day. But her husband, a miner, had been killed in a mine accident in Wales. When that happened poor Gladys ran as far away from Wales as she could, and now she lived in this nice little house down by the sea. Sometimes she did give a performance in a private house or in a hall, although recently she was bothered with cystitis and had

* clootie dumpling – a dumpling wrapped in cloth and boiled

become slightly incontinent in her old age. So, maybe she would start singing, then suddenly, cross-legged and in a great flurry, her beads round her neck swishing backwards and forwards across her ample bosoms, she would try to make a graceful exit, her legs crossed like a pair of scissors. But she would still get tremendous applause, everyone appreciated her and loved her very dearly.

When she saw Fran she took an instant liking to her. When she was told that Fran was now orphaned and all about the fire in the manse, she wondered what she could do for the girl. She offered to give her employment – helping her around the house – and what was better still, she decided to make her some clothes. Gladys Featherstone was remarkable in that there was nothing she couldn't make! She made her own soap, all her own clothes, got the wool off her own sheep, spun it on her spinning wheel. Her loom she'd made herself with the help of a local lad, so that she could weave, tailor, make paint, in fact I think there was nothing she couldn't do! She made many things to be sent to the War abroad, for the soldiers – blankets, camouflage – she was very much appreciated. So, Fran was fortunate that Gladys liked her so much. And she offered to finish off her education, teach Fran to read interesting books, play the piano, sewing, knitting, and helped her in many, many ways.

For it so happened that Gladys was related to the folk in the big house*; her mother at the time of her birth had been very ill and it was Fran's grandmother who was called in, to breastfeed the child. So, when Gladys remembered all these stories she had heard in the past, she took a strong liking to the little girl, eventually adopting her. Our Fran had the best of both worlds! She could still visit and be happy, spend days with Màiri Bhàn, and the rest of her time with Gladys Featherstone.

* big house – principal dwelling of the local landlord

The Druid Tree

Today was Sunday. This meant Gagach (the Stutterer) had to
go to church with his grandmother, and he was none too keen
to go. He'd been busy studying a grub make its way up into a
pear tree that was fixed to the high wall in his grandmother's
garden; pinned up against the wall like a fan, it had quite a bit
of fruit. Gagach was gazing spellbound at the little grub
climbing its way over a pear making a hole in the peel, trying
to work its way laboriously into the centre of the fruit.
Somehow or other this reminded him of himself. Nobody
wanted him, nobody cared, he was constantly teased and
mocked because of his stuttering; all he ever wanted to do
was hide or bury himself where nobody could ever find him.

He liked his grandmother very much and was an obedient
boy. So, when they made their way along to the village
church, he would let her think he was going to go in to
the service himself. But of course he had no intention of doing
so. He would see his grandmother off at the gate of the
church, tell her he was going to join the lads up in the balcony,
which she of course could not do since she was well into her
eighties. As soon as he got her settled in the church he would
sneak off, make his way down to the river and there hide under
the bridge until the service was over. The best of it was, he
could hear the service, the sound seemed to be amplified
under the bridge. He loved the music, the psalms, especially
the Twenty-third Psalm, all sung in Gaelic. He'd learned a
little Gaelic from his grandmother and the words fascinated

him, the moaning, chanting in Gaelic was spellbinding to his ears: 'A ta e 'ga mo threòrachadh, gu mìn réidh anns gach ball' (Yea, though I walk by the still waters).

The still waters, that was him – sitting here by the waters, only they weren't very still. There was a rapid flow, but music in it all round him. And he found it quite difficult to rouse himself when he knew the service was over, make his way to the front of the church, where his grandmother would find him and ask in Gaelic how he liked the sermon, 'Ciamar a bha an searmon a' cordadh riut?'

And he would say in Gaelic, 'Glé mhath, 's e bha math' (very well, it was very good). And they would make their way home to a good hot dinner.

Now, Gagach and his father had come to live with his grandmother when Gaggie's mother died. At the same time his father had retired from the Merchant Navy. He was now an old seadog, ready for retirement because he had injured his back, no doubt with the hard work he'd done all his grown life in the Navy. He was a tough guy and wanted his son to be the same. Unfortunately, Gagach, or Gaggie as they called him, was not of the same temperament. He was a dreamer, a bit of a poet, and his father despaired of him ever being a real man. So, he equipped him with ropes and gear, got him to take an interest in climbing the Cuillins in Skye to see if it would toughen him up. Failing that, he would have to send him to Leith, to a training ship that took on young lads and toughened them up, hired them out frequently to yachts which came in and wanted an extra hand for cruising or sailing around the Hebridean islands. And this old Angus thought was the ideal place to send his son.

Meanwhile, the granny was delighted to have the pair of them staying with her. She adored her son Angus, did everything she could to make him really comfortable, cosseted him and attended to his sore back; she even had a special wicker chair made for him, an enormous affair that had been made in the north end of Skye in Kilmuir to take his enormous bulk. And he would sit there of an evening cutting his black twist tobacco against the palm of his thick-skinned hand, rubbing and caressing it, filling his briar pipe. It fascinated young Gagach, because he'd never seen a lid on a pipe before. His father explained to him that when the sea was very rough and the winds blowing hard, it was possible that the tobacco would be swept out; so this special lid with a perforated top safeguarded his tobacco.

At the end of that summer Angus gave young Gaggie his own seagoing suitcase of green canvas, and advised him to go and fit himself up with a pair of brown shoes; 'All the best sailors,' he said, 'wore brown shoes with their navy blue or black mufti clothes.' So young Gaggie went off, bought himself a fine pair of brown shoes and travelled south by himself to Leith.

He was very sad leaving his grandmother and his father; now that he had no mother he felt terribly alone in the world. Leith seemed to him a very austere, grim and cold place. The training ship was also very frightening. They were strict on board and the lads all had to work hard wasting no time at all. 'Five minutes before time is navy time,' they would say, 'and everything must be spick and span.' So Gaggie worked very hard and had little leisure for the first month. Then he got more friendly with some of the lads, they tolerated his stuttering and ceased to make fun of him. He joined them to go ashore, found out where the best pubs were. There was one in particular that Gaggie liked best. It had a wee room apart from the bar they called 'the situterie'. It had velvet seats, was triangular in shape and meant for people to get away from the crowd, converse, or play cards; or, if they were lucky enough to find a girlfriend – maybe they would canoodle for a wee while. And so, Gaggie would go in there, usually by himself and simply contemplate, dream about being back home in Skye. This went on for some months, when one day he was sitting there quietly, a young lady walked in hopping on one leg and holding on to the lintel of the door. 'What's the trouble?' Gaggie asked.

And she said in broken English, 'I t'ink I have got a, er, pebble or stone in my shoe. It very sore.' So he helped her sit down beside him on the plush, red velvet cushion, helped her to take her shoe off. Sure enough there was a pebble in it.

And he sympathised with her while he took a good look at her long slim legs in their silk stockings, and thought, 'She's not a bad looker this one!' But it was going to be awkward because he couldn't quite make out what she was saying.

Then she explained that she was French, actually an au pair working for a doctor, his wife and two children nearby, that she'd got some time off, went for a walk and suddenly got this pebble in her shoe. And it was, 'Oh, très malheureusement.' Well, Gaggie didn't know what that meant, but he was pretty sure it was jolly sore. And so she rested there for a while, he bought her a drink.

Gradually he began to make out what she was talking about, she seemed to understand him very well, so they made a date for the following evening. This became a habit and they saw quite a lot of each other from then on. But, perhaps fortunately for Gaggie, the relationship could not last much longer. He was keen enough, but she seemed to be slackening off; when he arranged to meet her she would be an hour late, have some paltry excuse or other, and he was getting very peeved. He still believed that he'd grown fond of her, even that he loved her.

So this was upsetting for her. She was a very lovely-looking girl, but an outrageous flirt. He put that down to her being

French, because rightly or wrongly he'd come to believe that French women were like that. She would flirt with the other men at the bar when they met in the pub and he found this very, very hard to take. Late on in the year, Christmas time, it meant a lot for him to enjoy their company together. But once again, not only was she late, in actual fact she didn't appear at all. He waited and waited. There was no sign of her.

So he rang up the doctor's house where he knew she worked. They said they didn't know where she was, she ought to have been in at ten o'clock, the regulation in their household, and there was no sign of her. So Gaggie thought the best thing to do was to walk along to the house where she worked, wait for her. He strolled along sadly and slowly till he got to the house. He rang the bell, the doctor himself answered.

He said, 'We don't know what's happened to her. My wife had a look in her room and found that her suitcase had gone, all her clothes, it looked as if she'd disappeared altogether. She's left no note, we are completely handicapped with the children and everything; we've been in touch with the police, they haven't seen or heard of her. And the whole business is a complete disaster.'

So Gaggie turned away miserably and thought the only thing he could do was to get back to the pub, wait there; he went into the wee situterie with a large whisky and waited. He was already adrift now, as they were supposed to be in before midnight on board ship. So after several whiskies and feeling very drunk – he waited till after dark – he thought he could sneak aboard without being seen. But a very officious, Irish petty officer saw him climbing aboard and gave him hell.

'What's your excuse?' he said.

And Gaggie muttered out with his stutter, 'I've b-b-been to mi-mi, mi-mi-mi-midnight mass, sir.'

The officer was furious, sent him below decks and the

following day was determined to punish him by giving him a frightful lot of extra work to do. He had to polish all the nautical instruments, scrub decks; then he was asked to scrub the small crafts that belonged to the ship one after the other, six small boats, scrub them all out. Well, Gaggie did the first one, totally exhausted, and with a frightful hangover had a go at doing the next one, and then the third one. Then something happened to him. His mind went blank, he stood up, flung down the mop and stared at the petty officer. They were tied up along the quayside, so it was easy for him to jump ashore, which he did.

The petty officer yelled at him, 'Come back! Halt! Halt, halt! I only say it three times. If you don't I shoot.' He waves his gun in the air prepared to shoot him in the back. But Gaggie is stone cold with no feeling whatsoever in his body or his mind. He just strides on like a zombie till he reaches the gates taking no notice of the officer.

Gaggie didn't know what had come over him, why he was going or where. He just knew he must go. He didn't bother reporting his jumping ship to any authority, just bought a rail ticket for Inverness when he reached Waverley station. Of course he took the train from Inverness to Kyle of Lochalsh, and the ferry home. He didn't know what his father or his grandmother would say when he turned up like that, with no explanation and no word. But I suppose it would be clear to them that he was ill. Allette, his girlfriend in Leith, had caused him acute depression. He couldn't master it, felt all the time that he wanted to cry. Well, men don't cry, especially sailors. His father would be disgusted.

But in fact when he arrived at their doorstep back home, his father grinned from ear to ear. All he said was, 'Well, lad, it's well seeing it wasn't the Merchant Navy – you wouldn't have got away with it.'

And his grandmother gave him an enormous hug, sat him down to a warm and comforting meal. But this depression didn't go away. Constantly he thought about Allette, wondered where she was and why she'd done this. All the time his mind was worrying about her, perhaps he had said something or done something to offend her. But then she would have reacted against him. She hadn't. She'd just vanished. So he collected his climbing gear, spent most of his time walking up the hills relaxing in the mountains, then would come back home dead tired.

But on his way home there was a tree that comforted him greatly. He didn't know what kind, but he was certain in his mind that it was some sort of sacrificial tree. He knew in fact that it was a druid tree, but he didn't know how he knew. He had heard of a life-sized carving of a female figure in a peat bog near Ballachulish from the nineteenth century, possibly taken from a tree trunk . . . 'Just like yours, yes, a sacrificial wooden carving. But I have nothing to offer in a sacrifice but myself,' and he talked to it. He would ask its advice and in a strange way it seemed to answer him. He didn't know whether the tree spoke Gaelic or if it spoke an earlier language, or if indeed it spoke at all.

And this particular day, laden with his heavy gear, boots and rope, he took a look at the branches and said to himself, 'Why should I continue on home, why shouldn't I just stay here? Talk to the tree for a while, then maybe try out the branches for my weight?' He didn't realise he was contemplating suicide. But in fact he was. He thought he would try French first, he knew a little; after all, Allette was a French girl, maybe the tree could get a message to her. So he said over and over again, 'Si cher cher poor Allette, si cher cher poor Allette, si cher cher poor Allette.'

But there was no sound from the tree, just a sort of

crackling in its branches. No words came. And no words came into his head that might have come from the tree.

So he bashed on with Gaelic. He bashed on with Gaelic very politely, 'Ma 's e ur toil e,' he said, 'ma 's e ur toil e, cait a bheil Allette, cait a bheil Allette?'*

But there was still no reply. So then he decided that he would try his weight on the tree. As he moved up . . . one branch, that was steady enough . . . and then another. And then the tree seemed to hiss a sound into his ears like tinnitus, which he'd heard of, a sort of humming sound. It seemed to be saying in Gaelic, 'Stad ort, stad ort, stad ort!' (That means, wait, you wait, wait!) But he ignored it, flung the rope over a much higher branch – from which he'd made up his mind to hang himself.

When suddenly the tree began to shake vigorously; it nearly threw him off and he heard coming from the sea the sound of shouting and yelling. He realised that somebody was shouting, 'Help, help, help!'

Instinctively he fell to the ground, threw off his boots, flung off his outer clothes, retained the rope and dived in. He was a great swimmer, loved swimming. So, strongly he shot out into the deep water and gradually the shouting grew louder as he swam nearer and nearer the craft. Eventually he got there and exhausted hung on to the gunwales. There were people on board, a man, a woman and a girl. They said the outboard engine on the boat was stalled, they had no oars or any way of getting back to the shore and unfortunately they couldn't swim. So poor old Gaggie, exhausted and all as he was, gave them the end of the rope, got it fixed and started to swim back towing the boat behind him.

It was no easy task, and he wavered first to starboard, then

* Ma 's e ur toil e, cait a bheil Allette – If you please, where is Allette?

to port. Eventually he made it to a bit of the shore he knew full well, as many a time he had played there, swam from there, and he knew the terrain very well indeed. So he made fast the rope to the tree and helped these three people ashore. Their gratitude had no measure. They tumbled out, hugged and kissed him, made such a huge fuss of him! They said their car wasn't far away, they insisted he come back home with them, have a warm bath, a meal and a good dram. He didn't have time, was so disorientated he had not taken a look at the girl. The mother and father, if that's what they were, were making such a fuss of him that he hadn't even given her a glance. But when he did – by golly! He'd thought Allette was a good-looking girl, but this one, they called her Griselda, she was a right bobby-dazzler. He had never seen anything so lovely in his entire life.

Gaggie didn't hesitate in taking up their warm invitation. How could he? How could he miss the opportunity of getting to know better the simply gorgeous Griselda! And Mr Saunders himself was very interested in Gaggie. None of them seemed to notice that he had a stutter. In fact, all the excitement and the drama, the shock, seemed to have not exactly cured him, but left him with just a faint stutter which, if anything, was rather attractive. Or, so Griselda said when she got to know him better. They became very firm friends. Mr Saunders insisted on taking Gaggie into his business, a building firm. He was a very prosperous man with a beautiful home; he and his wife made Gaggie feel so very much at home – they treated him from then on like a son. And Griselda treated him like a brother, unfortunately. He would have liked a deeper relationship, but that was not to be. Her sights were set higher, and although they had a lot in common, loved each other's company, they never married. But they did remain the best of pals for all time to come.

Seeing is Believing

It was a cold January afternoon when the steamers left Mallaig; one for the Outer Isles, the other for Skye. Curstag had almost got on the wrong one, for at low tide you can't see the names on the sides of the steamers. She had boarded one of them in a sort of a trance and gone below, led by the smell of fresh herring cooking. She hadn't had a fresh herring for years . . . and she hadn't been home for years either.

Home . . . how she had missed it. How she had scraped and striven to get enough together to pay for her fare, how little they knew, her parents, what she had been through – their optimistic letters congratulating her on her fine job, envying her fine friends, and fine digs. How little they knew. The fine job had folded months ago, she had trodden the streets from agent to agent trying everything from selling cosmetics to driving a milk van. The most luxurious digs she had ever known was the YWCA, and her only true friend had been a budgerigar; when it died the bottom fell out from her barrel and she wrote to tell them she was coming home.

How would they receive her? Not too well she feared – in this pensive and uncertain mood she found herself boarding a ship and going below to get her first meal for more than twenty-four hours. Then it was that she asked the steward what time she could expect to arrive in Skye? And he had politely told her that they did not touch Skye; in fact, they were bound for the Outer Isles on a round trip.

Grabbing her things together Curstag only just managed to

scramble off the ship in time. And now she was well underway on the right one, the ship that was bringing her nearer and nearer to home. As she stood on deck absorbing the landmarks that had filled her dreams for three long years she was struck by the beauty of the early evening sky – she had never seen it so beautiful, the orange and grey glow pierced by gleaming rays like swords of light thrusting out to the silhouette of crofters' houses edging the tops of the hills. One of these houses was hers and as the steamer got closer in the sunbeams seemed to settle on her house and the light on the windows was signalling a message to her . . . Ach, it could only be her imagination; she was tired, uneasy and deeply worried. How could she explain herself, admit to everyone that she had been a failure; for a moment she thought about turning back. Yes, she would just go back, but dash it all, someone was sure to have seen her so near and yet so far. She was trembling now, agitated and afraid.

Meanwhile they had come right alongside the pier, the lines were thrown out, the engines had stopped and there was a silence that nearly hurt. She could see the sunlight still dancing on the windows of her home and, as she drew nearer labouring with her luggage up her father's croft, she distinctly saw the words 'The Lord is my shepherd' written across the gleaming glass of the window. She stood for a moment transfixed, hypnotised; then a great feeling of relief surged through her. Her arms relaxed and her fingertips tingled. She felt strong and real, there was no longer any doubt in her mind, she was home.

Curstag never mentioned any of this to anyone (it was private), not until one evening round about the same time of year her mother came in from the milking white as a ghost – she had seen the words on the window too and she kept the secret close, in her heart.

Curstag and her mother had never what you might call 'hit it off' in the past, but now a strange bond seemed to be growing between them. It wasn't until they got a grant from the Board of Agriculture to extend their croft and make alterations that the mystery of the lettering revealed itself.

Curstag's father wanted to make a door instead of the front window, and as he was gently removing the glass he turned to Curstag and her mother and said, 'Well, it's funny that neither of you ever missed the glass from that old sampler in all these years.'

'What sampler?' said Curstag, lifting her hands from the baking and shaking the flour from them.

'Why, the one in the bedroom that says "The Lord is my shepherd". I used the glass to mend the pane I broke celebrating, the night you were born.'

'Let me see that glass,' said Curstag. And sure enough, if you turned it sideways you could still see the words 'The Lord is my shepherd' engraved with age and peat smoke right into the glass. Not that Curstag ever wanted to go back to the big city again, because once you've seen the light you know where the green pastures are – or should do.

Goosie Goosie Gander

Padraig was a poacher, and what's worse, a non-believer. He didn't believe in miracles or fairies or Santa Claus, Beecham's powders or the British Empire, or anything. There was no pleasing him. Then one day, he was talking to a cailleach who was tramping her washing in the burn. He jumped in beside her to give her a hand (or a couple of feet, I should say) with the washing, and it was then that she began to lecture him.

'Listen, laddie,' she said, 'if you believe in something, anything, anything at all, it is better than nothing. Nothingness is soul destroying . . .'

'Ach, duin do chlab,' (shut your trap) said Padraig. He was awful coarse, mind you, and she was awful angry.

So she splashed him out from the burn with a wet chemise (semmit) shouting, 'Mark my words, you'll be in jail before the night is out, you uncouth amadan!' Well, naturally enough, that was the last thing he would be believing, so he went on his way whistling.

Now, at the time he was going steady with a young chambermaid up at the big house, and she kept nattering on at him to marry her. 'How can I when I haven't a penny to my name?' he'd say.

The young caileag was none too honest, and unfortunately her need to marry him became more and more urgent as time went on. So when she found a broken necklace on the floor of the mistress's bedroom, the precious stones all scattered about, she took them up in the pocket of her pinny and slunk outside with them. She ran down towards the sea and hid them hurriedly in the long grass at the edge of the machair, marking the place with a stone, then went back to her work.

Now that same evening as the sun was crawling down under the hills Padraig went walking along the shore and took a pot at a wild goose rising from the machair, thinking to have it for his supper. Well, you can imagine his surprise when he came to pluck and draw and truss it to find inside its gullet a handful of precious stones. (He had heard of grouse and woodcock eating stones, but never a wild goose.) 'A strange bird,' he muttered scratching his head. Now, unlike his caileag, Padraig was no thief, poaching being just a pastime for him. So he wrapped the stones carefully in a newspaper and took them down to where the policeman was; and no sooner did he show the stones than they clapped the handcuffs on him and started to mock him mercilessly, chanting daft verses at him, like,

> Goosie goosie gander
> Whither shall I wander
> Upstairs and downstairs
> And in my lady's chamber.

Then they'd start roaring with laughter, give him a poke in the ribs and continue,

> There I met a young lad
> Who wouldn't say his prayers,
> I took him by the left leg
> And threw him down the stairs.

Then they charged him with breaking into the big house and stealing valuable jewellery.

He was struggling violently and protesting his innocence, when the old cailleach happened to be passing by: 'What did I tell you, young fella?' she squawked. 'If you don't learn to believe other people, how do you expect them to believe you?'

The Face in the Pool

There was a lad in Lower Breakish once, a bit of a simpleton they said. He lived with his granny and his uncle, and the boys at the school used to tease him so much that he got timid and scared. Then they would throw stones at him making him only worse, so he was afraid to go to school at all. He would leave home all right and wander about till it was time to go back again, and when his uncle found out he would thrash him with a five-fingered tawse that hung on the wall behind his chair.

One day he was wandering about and came up on the disused well that was on the lower end of his father's croft where his own home had once been. He knelt down idly beside it to clear the moss and frog spawn off the top of it, and instead of seeing his own reflection in the water he saw that of his father.

He was so astonished he nearly ran away, for his father, you see, had been dead for two years or more . . . He found he could hardly move, he was numb with fear . . . then he heard his father's voice in the wind saying, 'Stand up to them, boy! Don't be afraid, I am with you. Go now.' And feeling much bolstered by his beloved father's encouragement, he turned up at the school in the break time and lammed into the lot of them – thumping and jumping and laying them all flat one after the other.

It was a huge success, the boys were actually afraid of him now. And as time went on he grew stronger in himself and became quite a hero, as well as a very good scholar. But he never forgot the well and his father's voice; and although he would sit for hours stirring the water with his fingers, he never heard another cheep.

Till one day when he was fully grown and had decided to become a medical missionary, he asked his uncle to lend him enough money to go to the university in Glasgow but the old skinflint wouldn't part with a brass farthing. So what was he to do?

He wandered down once again to the old well on his father's croft to ruminate over the matter. It was a mild evening with a glowing sunset and as he looked into the shining water he saw a hand beckoning to him. He felt impelled to reach out for it; he wasn't afraid any more, but he was heavy now and rather clumsy and the stones at the side of the well gave way under the weight of his knee so that his hand and arm were thrust deep into the water, and his fingers, bruised with the jolt, closed round something that felt like metal discs. Yes, that's right, they were sovereigns . . . and enough to take him to Glasgow or Timbuktu for that matter. And that in fact is where he finally went, Timbuktu, as a missionary. And although he was grateful to the memory of his father he always referred to his find in the well as a 'gift of God'.

The Silo

The hay-cart was more a wagon than a cart; it lay against a big fishing boat tarred black and acted as a shelter for the peats mainly, but when it was empty the sheep would use it. They would squat in there on bad days when there was a howling wind coming through the mountains and through the trees till it reached the old boat. The mountains were huge and huddled in the distance, the Cuillin Hills, and the wind came howling through the cleavage of Beinn na Caillich and Blà Bheinn.* So no wonder, when the peats were not kept in this carvel old boat, the sheep would use it, leaving their droppings en masse all over the muddy floor.

The boat was so old that sphagnum moss – green, short, pretty stuff – had begun to grow in the grooves, on little ledges of the carvel old wood. Everything was very damp, helped along, mind you, by Iain Mór himself when he would sometimes come out in a hurry, be caught short and add his pee to the dripping boat. On this particular day he had been scything a whole field, stopping only to sharpen his blade with a stone he had for that purpose. He was exhausting himself, red in the face and perspiring like a bull. He simply must get the hay-cart filled up before the evening set in. He was absolutely furious with Paddy: Paddy was a man who had approached him not long ago for a job. He'd come over from Ireland, nobody knew anything about him. But Iain Mór

* Beinn na Caillich and Blà Bheinn – peaks in the Red Cuillins

thought he must just take a chance on it because there was far too much work to be done. He didn't at all like the look of the fellow, he was very short and very small and very sneaky-looking. He couldn't give any history or background for himself, he couldn't say which part of Ireland he came from or tell if he had ever done any job of any kind before, let alone a farming job. And even though Iain Mór was suspicious of him he really had nobody else he could fall back on to help him out.

He must hurry back home now with the hay-cart, previously filled, because his sweetheart, the lovely Annag, was coming to collect him. She was going to take him home to her people to discuss their engagement: they were now betrothed, very much in love, and final arrangements would have to be made for their wedding. Annag was lovely to look at, her hair glinted in the sun and then would turn in the shade to a coppery brown. Her eyes were the colour of bluebells, her skin whiter than milk. He adored her. So, he would have to hurry home.

He got inside and started to wash, change his clothes and shave. This was a labour he didn't much enjoy but it was a special occasion; he started with the right side with his cut-throat razor, gently steered round his ear, the side of his nose, round his lips, and was just about to tackle the other side of his face when he heard Annag's sweet voice singing as she came, dancing down the croft to join him. And then, before he started on his chin on the other side of his face he heard arguing. Then he heard shouting and he heard his own name being shouted.

'Iain, Iain, trobhad seo, trobhad, trobhad Iain!' (which means, Iain, come quick, come quick, come quick!)

He heard scuffling, then he heard a scream. He threw down his razor and raced out of the house, minus his trousers, just in his long johns – to find Paddy had lifted Annag up in his arms and flung her on to the hay-cart. He was now on top of her, had stripped and ripped her beautiful dress and was commencing to attack her. He'd squeezed her face down into the hay so that she was half smothered, unable to shout again. And Iain Mór, livid and infuriated fit to bust, grabbed a hold of the bastard's legs, and hauled him to the ground. He kicked the living daylights out of him, then pulling him to his feet he shouted to Annag, 'Go home, girl, go home!' And this she did, she ran like the wind in the direction of her mother's house. Iain Mór gripped the Irishman by the throat and contemplated throttling him to death, but thought the better of it. He thought to himself, 'Why should I do this, why should I murder the bastard? I'll see to it that he murders himself!'

With that he grabbed a piece of handy rope attached to the wagon, flung it round his neck and hauled the little man. He was easy enough to haul, shove, push; and Iain took him for at least half a mile up the croft to where he had recently invested in a silo, a magnificent ten-foot tall silo for holding the fodder for the winter, for his animals. They were met by a herd of Highland cattle, splendid with their tawny brown long coats and immense horns. A fearsome sight – one of them was an albino, pure white with fierce pink eyes. It was difficult driving them away, at the same time propelling the wee man through the entrance of the silo.

But having got the Irishman to the threshold of this fine building he pulled him inside, steered him towards the iron ladder that led up to a pigeon loft on the very top of the silo. Step by step he shoved the wretch's feet onto the spars of the iron ladder. The man was screaming and delirious, swearing and wetting himself and in a terrible state. But Iain Mór didn't care. Step by step he propelled him up and up, up to the very top of the pigeon loft. It was a very dangerous position for the pair of them to be in, even the coorie doos, the wee pigeons, were scared out of their wits and flew away through the hole up into the sky. Because Iain Mór's threats and language were petrifying. He shook the little man, screaming, 'Mhic an Sad, amadain, cachd bhàn mise stad thusa*!' and was shaking the man; and the slippy droppings of the pigeons on a ledge they were standing on – the little fellow slid and fell over the edge – down, down he went. Not slowly like a parachute, but like a ton of beef. And the thud on the cement face of the base made a noise like thunder. It was more than likely his brains would be scattered all over the cement floor. It was horrifying.

Iain Mór found it difficult to contain himself. He was dizzy, thought he would fall, thought he would follow the fellow, but gripping hold of a bar he managed to steady himself enough and gradually made his way down the iron steps. The fellow was dead all right and what a mess. Now what must he do? What on earth must he do? The police would have to be told; would he be considered a murderer? He started to vomit, and then forced himself to stagger through the doorway and out into the open air. He wasn't real, he wasn't himself, he was someone else. He hadn't done it, he hadn't done anything, though God knows he wanted to. He didn't know how to take this, he didn't know how to go home. He made for the river and stuck his head in the deep water till he nearly choked. And then he thought maybe he'd better have choked. Was he a murderer? Was it an accident? What would they say?

He sat on a boulder at the side of the river suffering from cold guilt and mortification all night long till it became pitch dark. Demons will sulk and mourn while angels rejoice in heaven. And then gradually the light dawned in more ways than one. He'd been resting with his back against the branch

* Mhic an Sad, amadain, cachd bhàn mise stad thusa – son of Satan, idiot, I will put an end to your filth

of a tree, a rowan tree, and somehow that seemed to give him courage and inspiration.

He realised that Annag would have arrived home in a terrible state and that she would have told her mother; her mother then would tell her father exactly what happened to her, and her father would be incensed. The first thing he would want to do as soon as daylight dawned would be to contact the police. None of them knew who this fellow was, the only clue they had was that he was Irish. And when Annag's father got in touch with the police they told him that they had been searching for a member of the IRA, wanted by the police in this country, wanted badly by the Gardai in Ireland. This was by no means his first offence. He'd raped and he'd murdered, was badly wanted, to be punished. But now there was no doubt about it; he was dead.

So the report would be given: his fear of being captured caused him to make his way into Iain Mór's silo and commit suicide. And that would be the end of it. That, fortunately was the end of it. There were many rumours going about – did he fall or was he pushed? Nobody could give the answer to that, except of course the coorie doos in the pigeon loft.

And there we can add, through time, Annag and her Iain Mór managed to put the episode out of their minds, because there was to be a great banquet and a wonderful céilidh. The eightsome reels, the jigs and the dancing would go on for at least three days, so it would all be out of their system in no time at all.

Heart of Stone

Ploughing his way through the soggy croft that was pitted with the hoof-marks of starving animals, Donald Crùbach protected the bundle of groceries he was bringing home from the shop – an ample supply because he was hungry. But then so were his animals, however this didn't worry Donald. For it was well known in the district that all his sheep were dying from starvation. There were corpses lying on the shore, or falling down the cliffs and into the bogs from sheer weakness. His stirks also were known to be fed on a couple of handfuls of bruised oats, or oil cakes which he carried in his pocket and distributed as though he were feeding hens.

Yes, Donald was a hard-hearted man and the folk round about had had just about enough of him. He had never been known to do a good turn for anybody. So nobody cared two hoots when one day he completely disappeared. Months went by and there was no sign of him. 'Maybe the banshee got him,' you would hear them say. The last time anyone saw him was down on the shore gathering spout-fish (for himself, of course) and talking to a wee bent old woman. 'Oh, that would be the banshee right enough,' they said; and so indeed it was.

Donald had been gathering spout-fish, or trying to, at least, but even they were avoiding him, squelching back into the sand before he could get a right hold on them. It was then that a squeaky voice said to him, 'Would you give me one or two for my dinner? My back is that bad I can't bend the way I used to.'

'No,' said Donald crossly, 'I'm having enough difficulty catching the blighters myself.'

'Well,' said the cailleach, 'you're getting them for nothing, aren't you? You ungrateful amadan, and I think it's about time you got a bit of a lesson – a heart of stone is no good to man or beast. So I think I'll just cast a spell on you, until your heart melts once more. Then I will release you.'

With that she raised her stick, then, making three figures of eight in the sand she spat in the middle of each circle and stood staring at Donald as he grew smaller and smaller, his hard features rigid with fear. As she continued to work on him he became more and more solid till at last he was nothing but a small-sized boulder – nicely marked, mind you. And there she left him.

Now through time, as he didn't return home, Donald's brother decided to sell the croft; it was bought by a Sassenach lady who wanted to get away from it all. In a very short time she converted the tumble-down croft house into a nice cosy dwelling – and she was a nice cosy wee woman herself, with a kind and generous nature.

One sunny afternoon she decided to go down to the shore to select one or two nice stones to make a fireplace with. And it was then that she saw a small boulder with nice markings on it – just the very thing she wanted for the centre of the fireplace. So with some difficulty she rolled it home and got it cemented in just under the mantle shelf. It looked quite charming, she thought. Soon she was able to light a fire, and, as she sat of an evening, she would admire the stone and got quite fond of it. As she was very lonely, she would find herself talking to it, just as though it were a human being. The sort of things she was saying were soft and gentle, kind and loving, things poor Donald had never heard spoken in all his natural life.

Gradually, he began to respond and he could feel himself, his heart of stone, melting by the sound of her kind words and the warmth of the fire. For the first time he regretted his past and knew that if he could only have another chance he would be the kindest, most considerate man that ever lived. And somehow or other the banshee must have got to know of this, for she relented.

One night, after the lady had gone to bed and the fire had smouldered out, she came slithering down the chimney and started her figure of eight design on the hearth. Only this time in the reverse direction, and no spits. It worked quite well and Donald was back to himself, again, only better-looking – and no longer crùbach – bent, crooked.

Well, as you can imagine the lady was very disturbed in the morning when she came down to find a strange man in her sitting room. 'What are you doing in my house?' said she to him.

'What are you doing in my house?' said he to her. And after much deliberation and argy-bargy, the matter was amicably resolved. For the Sassenach lady agreed to become co-owner of the house and contented wife of Donald, who, after all, had got the best of the bargain as he now had someone on whom he could lavish all his newfound love and affection. Nach robh sin anabarrach – wasn't that amazing and wonderful!

Fair Exchange

Màiri MacKinnon's shop? Ach, you know it fine. It used to be a sweetie shop selling aniseed balls. It's up the Entry Mór past the elm tree at the corner of the dyke. Did you know it was once a tailor shop, though? Years ago that is, before the war – the Boer War of course – well, it was!

Màiri MacKinnon had three sons, you see. One a tailor, one a sailor and the other an excise man. The oldest one decided to become a tailor because it was the duty of the eldest son to stay home and mind the croft, his mother being a widow an' all, and the poor fellow had no fancy for it. He didn't take to the outdoor work at all, he being a bit of a scholar – self-taught, mind you, and very shrewd. He struck on the idea of building a lean-to (annexe) to the house and of learning a trade that would keep him at home and enable him to have an eye on the croft at the same time. Well, he was out of luck! Come the war and there was nobody wanting suits at all; they were all into the regimental kilt, and the tartan trews supplied by the army, himself included.

So with the tailor and the sailor away at the war, Màiri decided the only thing she could do with the lean-to was to make it into a sort of general store, for she was a shrewd one also, you understand! She bought everything in bulk as fine she knew that as time went on there was sure to be a shortage. She stocked up with meal and flour, tea and cocoa, to say nothing of aniseed balls and Madeira cake, and if her son the excise man wasn't about, who knows, you might have got a

44

drop of the hard stuff (for medicinal purposes only, of course). Yes, Màiri was the wise one and the energetic one, she thought nothing of walking a good nine miles to select her barrels of flour, Russian flour marked 'X0X Superfine' that used to come in with the fishing fleet in those days. There were boats from France and Russia and Denmark galore – when the herring fishing was so plentiful – and sometimes there would be quite a spot of confusion on the quayside, none of the foreigners speaking the Gaelic, you see. So Màiri would just point her finger at the barrels she wanted and smile, and if she hadn't enough money she would maybe pay them with eggs or chickens.

Well, one morning after paying one of the Russians for her flour, she gave him a beautiful smile and a packet of aniseed balls; and after she had got back home and the carrier had delivered her goods, she started to open the barrels. She discovered to her amazement that one of them was full to the brim with tobacco – tobacco, mind you, the price of it! That fool of a carrier had lifted the wrong one, surely? There was no 'X0X Superfine' on the side of it. It must be contraband, and her son an exciseman – what on earth was she to do?

'Well, when in doubt say nothing,' thought Màiri the shrewd one. Sleep on it, that's the thing.

And it was a good job she did, too, as by the time she got round to telling her son what had happened, it was too late for him to do anything at all about it; for the Russians had lifted anchor and were well on their way back home.

'Ach well,' thought Màiri, 'they wouldn't be missing a barrel of backy all that much, now would they?' And, after all, she had given them the aniseed balls.

The Changeling

Seumas was a wee man, some say he had been a changeling; everything about him was tiny, even his house had become round in the building of it since there was no space allowed to take the corners. The heavy thatch was also round with one chimney protruding at the side, like the cockade in a Balmoral. Wee and all as he was, he had to stoop low to get himself inside the door. Once inside the whole of the floor space was only six feet by six feet; nevertheless he had furnished it comfortably, a wooden bed filled with sweet-smelling hay, a well scrubbed table, and a trust, or sort of bench; there was a keisht in the window which served as a washstand, and he had made a couple of chairs to match his anatomy by carefully choosing bent tree branches that took the same curves as himself. His most useful possession was a wee three-legged cauldron. He was a great food fancier, as bachelors often are, and would go many miles to find something tasty; he sometimes went halfway up the mountain side for blaeberries.

He also collected small puinneags and herbs for soup, thistle heads for cheese and crabs, whelks and mussels galore – the wealthy English landowners and tourists had depleted his favourite oyster beds, but there were still a few to be found in the narrows between Strollamus and the Island of Scalpay at the ebb of the spring tide. Seumas would serve himself with these titbits with the delicacy of a well trained maitre d'hotel, using decorated wooden quaichs which he had carved himself and little clay pots for the soups and mushrooms, and believe it or not he ate with a gilded spoon! Now, only the bansìth herself could have given him that! He made a little hedgehog out of a cork fishing float, and its pine quills he used for eating the whelks for his supper; the tide was ebbing when he started collecting them, and he was so eager trying to fill his sack before nightfall that he didn't notice the tide creeping up on him.

He tried to get back home by crossing the narrows, but with the heavy sack he just wasn't quick enough and he soon submerged; then he let go the sack and rose to the surface (every drowning man rises at least once so they say) and there was no one about to hear his cries for help. But fortunately for him he was seen by a couple of porpoises frisking about, leaping and jumping joyously on the surface of the water.

Now, it is well known that porpoises have supernatural powers, and have always been the friends of man. So they swam underneath wee Seumas and propelled him back to land, one on either side like . . . like a catamaran. He lost all his whelks, of course, but then even a changeling can't have everything all his own way . . . or can he?

Skye Fever

Don't please run away with the idea that all we Highlanders hibernate in winter – far from it. There's more doing in winter in the Isle of Skye than the whole of Glasgow put together – the county council meetings, the debates and the arguments, the evangelists and the Mormons, the sewing class and the WRI, etcetera. There are times when one wonders where it will all end.

'Things is not what they used to be,' says one.

'Do you think it's for the best?' says another.

'Should they run the Sunday ferries, or not? Obh, obh.' (woe, woe)

'Should they lift the garbage in Uig and charge it through the rates?'

'The whole island's in a quandary.'

'They've had Ban the Bomb sit-downs on the pier at Kyleakin, and there's some talk of an air-strip being built at Aiseag.' (Get away!)

'They are putting a new wing to the White Heather Café in Kyleakin. Do you remember when it was just a shop that had once stored tar and rope and paint on the quayside; then it became a butcher's shop when the islanders couldn't get more than a couple of shillings a head for their sheep; and then a small tea shop? I went in there in one of those early days and they were so desperate to serve me quickly (a customer at last) that they didn't wait for the kettle to boil. There was a big pot already heated, out of which they had just taken a lobster. The tea tasted more like epsom salts than anything else. Not so today – they serve more than a hundred customers sometimes in the season. I went in to buy a hen. The Polish owner opened the deep freeze for me to select one.

'Dhis is a very good make,' he said. 'I can recommend it.'

'But I thought God made hens,' I said.

'Well, you couldn't have a more reliable source of supply, could you?'

'Mar e tha sibh cnàide!' (You've said it!)

'There's talk of extending the Broadford Hospital, too.'

'I heard that. Well, well.'

'Do you know that the fishermen are having to buy their fish as they need their boats for chartering trippers? They will have the best of both worlds anyway. If it's true what they're saying, that the distribution and selling of the big fish catches are to be done from Uig. They can buy the fish there and stick it in the deep freeze. They've got the salmon and crowdie in there already – no longer any need to preserve the meat with peat smoke (like old Seadan who used to hang a whole side of mutton on a hook above the chimney piece, and cut himself off a slice when he felt so inclined).

'An ainm an àigh!' (In the name of the Deity!) 'But somehow nowadays one doesn't seem to get so hungry any more, and things don't smell so good or so strong. We are choosey and liverish and seem to have lost the sense of smell. Even peat smoke and bog myrtle and seaweed are losing their pungent aroma. You have to use your nostrils like a direction finder or submarine radar and when you're on target, inhale with all your might; and in that way you might get a wee sniffle of Skye air instead of the diesel fumes from the buses.' 'Tha sin ceart!' (You're right there!)

'And who can make a caman for playing shinty?' (Who plays shinty?) 'And who can make a creel?' (What's a creel?)

'When did you last taste stapag?' (cream from the churn and oatmeal)

'Cream did you say? I think you'd have to order that from Inverness.'

When the wheel turns
The crannachan churns
And the song of the soup
Goes plup, plup, plup.

'Bi sàmhach!' (Belt up!)

The old man sits on his wooden chair
Bended and torn and rotted with fear
Fear of some monstrous dinosaur
From four-hundred thousand fathoms deep.

The old man sits on his fibreglass chair
His pep pill beside him, he hasn't a care
Hasn't a care, watching the telly
His feet in the air.

'Which is better?'
'Which is worse?'
'I like the television fine, but we're not getting a very good reception.'

'I'd rather go to the pictures; I like stamping my feet, and if I try it at home they all start hissing.'

'Ah, but is the television teaching us anything new – anything we didn't know before? You're forgetting a lot of us still have the second sight; and there are the books we can get through the book club. And I've yet to see a television play about a pair of lovers having their legs and hands tied by their parents before being chucked in the one bed and left to get on with it – there's imagination for you! Some of the ideas we Highlanders have would make *The Carpet Baggers* and *Fanny Hill* read like an income tax schedule!'

'Salachar.' (Big dirt!) 'What was that I was saying about smell, or rather the lost art of smelling? It was common practice in these parts (still is, I believe) to put the skin of a sheep who had died while bearing its lamb on to another mother sheep who had lost its lamb (if you follow me). By doing so, the little orphan lamb would smell the skin and think it was its own mother. Sometimes this works and the lamb can suckle away to its heart's content. And now the scientists are doing their best to fox us in much the same way. They are making fertiliser smell like horse manure, and horse manure smell like pine needles.'

'Well, I never, did you ever hear the like?'

'Dig that!'

'Time was when an old Clydesdale and a faded pink and blue cart would trundle up from the cladach, or shore, with a load of wet seaweed to spread on the ground as fertiliser, no matter what it smelt like. Now, I believe, seaweed is used by chemical factories for making meringues. No wonder they taste so lousy.'

'Get away! Says who?'

'There's an old Gaelic toast: 'Suas an fheamainn!' (which means, up with the seaweed; or, as we now say, 'Knock it back!') Of course, if it was the minister paying a call – 'Dean umbrella leis!' might be more refined. (Make an umbrella of it, or, turn it up!) And don't forget to give him a peppermint to take away the smell. Today, of course, it would be an Amplex pill* (for safe drivers).'

* Amplex pill – strong commercial peppermint

'My grand-uncle was reputed to be able to smell anybody coming up the croft a mile-and-a-half away.'

'Is that a fact? Well, well.'

'Get lost!'

'I was reading the other day (in a science magazine) that unattractive-smelling females lower the population amongst insects – that is, they tell us that the destructive caterpillars which shave the pine trees in the forests of their needles, reproduce themselves in billions.'

'Be quiet!'

'Belt up!'

'This means, then, that the prolific lady caterpillars when they become flies must be "humdingers" and smell divine.'

'Yeah, yeah . . . man, it's rave!'

'Perhaps it is due to all these discoveries about smell that we are given so many advertisements about BO on the television. It might be an idea to invent a special spray for spinsters or lonely bachelor girls. One thing leads to another, doesn't it?'

'Tha sin fìor!' (That is wicked!)

'And how!'

'The magazine suggests that the menace of birds to aircraft and fishermen can be minimised by using either loudspeakers transmitting the distress cries of the birds, or, temporarily paralysing them with microwaves.'

'Crìoch nam beann.' (Top of the mountain, unbelievable.)

'Way out, man, it's wide!'

'Can you imagine the fishermen gutting their fish with a flock of ruddy great herring gulls sitting on their heads and shoulders (unable to flutter a flap)? On the other hand, it might be a smashing way of catching poachers.'

'Mar e tha 's cnàide!' (As you say!)

'Dead right, mate!'

Skye Fever

Fasten your belts
You arrogant Celts
All those upstanding
Prepare for landing
For the time is soon
To drop on the moon.

'Do you think we are any better for being "with it"? I ask you, can a cigarette offered to you by the maintenance man who comes to mend your washing machine compare with the squeeze your grandmother got from Big Angus when she went down to the burn to boil her smalls in a cauldron? That's life. What's given by the one hand is taken away by the other.'

'Gu dearbh, gu dearbh.' (True, true.)

'Ask me another!'

'Not so long ago they used to think that science meant putting organs in churches or erecting telegraph poles. At any rate, it was a bad thing. One old boy used to use science as a threat before starting a fight. "Seall e mise sciance dhuibh!" he would shout (I'll show you science!) and give his unsuspecting opponent a knock-out blow. Why, even the geologists chipping away at the rocks were supposed by some to be tapping messages to old Nick himself.

'Bi falbh.' (Away with you!)

'Turn it up!'

'Do you know that when I was little, I discovered a link between the whole wide world and myself . . . it was a telegraph pole . . .'

'Bonkers!'

'Life is like a telegraph pole – a thing through which we mingle and pass. If you sit close up to one on a summer's day and press your ear to the warm wood you become part of it and a picture of the whole world comes before you; you know what people are doing and saying and you become afraid for them and for yourself, and you take yourself away to play a game of a different sort but you can't get the people out of your mind. There is an old clinker boat down by the shore turned upside down and near to it a clay-pit – white clay with fragments of shell in it. You make little people with it – dozens of them – and line them all along the grooves of the wooden boat to dry in the sun. But when you collect them again they crumble up in your hands and fall to pieces – "dust to dust".'

'As sure as death.'

'It's way out!'

'But for today's child the television is the mixer, the transmitter. Television is their link with the wide world and the wider beyond. They can become devoted worshippers. How then can they experience anything real for themselves? Not only will they lose all sense of taste and smell, they stand a very good chance of losing the use of their limbs as well. Give me a telegraph pole any day.'

'Steall ort.' (Stir it!)

'Wrap it up!'

'Nobody walks any more, except the hikers from the South, and the likes of Doctor Babs Moore. Whom did she meet as she stopped to eat her grass? Ghosts, perhaps? The ghost of my grandmother on her way to Perth (from Skye) walking, hell-bent on making a good business deal (flogging whisky in those days was a secret and confidential transaction). Did she meet the ghost of Flora MacDonald on horseback returning from Edinburgh, or maybe Fyfe Robertson living it up in the past, present and future? At any rate, no one needed Doctor Beeching's railroads* then, and it looks as though we could manage full well without them in the future, too (although I

* Doctor Beeching's railroads – the unpopular national organisation of British Rail

shouldn't say it). What with hovercraft and planes, etcetera –
why, only the other day I saw one of those amphibious cars,
and I couldn't help thinking the driver (my cousin Catriona)
looked kind of daft, grinning away complacently as she drove
straight off the road on to the sea, just like in a nightmare.'
 'Gu seallaibh Dhia.' (Good God!)
 'It's way out!'

> The Crusaders' bodies lie facing the East
> Tomorrow's pibroch laments for today;
> Maggots and mildew, midges and men
> Are with us, perhaps till the end.

'Calum Murchison, what's man's chief end?'
'Man's chief end is to glorify God and enjoy him forever.'
'Niste, put out your hand as I command – the teacher to obey!'
'You there, Computer, how many miles to the moon?'
'Fifty-thousand billion years, sir.'
'Wrong again, that was when life began.'
'Twenty-thousand billion miles, sir.
'Man, that's gear!'
'Did the prophet Brahan Seer say that that would be the end
of life? He must have been joking.'
'No, sir, the beginning.'
'The beginning of the end, you mean.'
'A'ghealach ag éirigh.' (The moon is rising.)

> The grey seal turns
> And its whiskers twitch
> But the Island sleeps on.

'Watch it, mate!'
'The Brahan Seer has told us this Island's fate:

It shall be overrun by rats
And swallowed back into the sea.

'Dhia beannaich sinn!' (God bless us!)
'Was his foresight dim, then?'
'When particles of man and mud are thrown in an atomic
rage, who can distinguish? Might we not run like rats?'
'Bi falbh!' (Get lost!)
'Sgapadh!' (Clear off!)
'Obh, obh!' (Woe, woe!)
'Drop dead!'
'Mix me a toddy, and let me to bed.'
'Oidhche mhath leibh!' (Good night to you!)
'Good night, all.'*

---

* This story, a bardic flyting, carries early predictions – might this
be the second sight?

Fantasies Apart

All on a Summer's Day

Once there was a drove of deer that used to munch its way through the long grass patches that grew in the valleys around Loch Hourn. The mountains surrounding this loch are mystical, gaunt and lonely. There are, however, one or two small shooting lodges, some isolated crofters' cottages dotted here and there, and every now and then a yacht sails in or a fishing boat. But the main feature of the place is the horned deer. At certain times of the year you can find cast-off antlers strewn around the edge of the loch. But it is not about these antlers I want to tell you; it's about the strange young lad who used to collect them and hollow them out to make whistles.

He lived with his parents in one of those abandoned little shooting lodges that his father had acquired just after the war. Moses (young Angus's father, so called on account of his long beard) was a shoemaker to trade and had his nameplate nailed to one of the two spiky ewe trees that supported an immense pair of stag's antlers crowning the entrance to his home. The interior of the house was wooden and warm, hung with sheep, otter and sealskins, many of which were used in his work. For he frequently made sporrans, and his gillie shoes with tassels on were famous at home and abroad. He was a skilled artist, there is no doubt, and so was his son. They would sit of an evening, the young Angus polishing his whistles and the old man treadling away on his old sewing machine under the watchful gaze of Makarios (his devoted collie dog).

Yes, young Angus had quite a gift for music, a bit of a bard you might say. He could most often be found lying on his stomach in the long grass or sitting on a lichen-covered lump of granite whistling out his tunes. The beautiful setting and surrounding mountains were not the source of his inspiration any more than for a boy raised in the back streets of Putney or Paisley; for tall mountains, tall chimneys or tall buildings are much the same anywhere if you half close your eyes. They can be flicked away and replaced by vast open spaces with cow-boys galloping, or tall spruce masts on a rolling sea . . . a pink clover sea, perhaps . . . was that a boat he could see coming up the loch? Or, was he dreaming again? He raised himself on his elbows to keek over the top of the grass for from here he could see without being seen.

Yes, it was a boat all right . . . a fast motor boat; it had better be fast, too, or they would never get out from here till the next tide. They must be strangers not to know that. Angus watched the boat move into the loch and throw an anchor without even sounding the depth. They must be daft. He wondered if he should shout to them, but they had already launched a dinghy and were coming ashore, or rather one of them was. A female. Angus didn't think she could ever have handled oars before, splashing about like one possessed. Suddenly, a couple of shots rang out, the deer grazing beside Angus hooked the air and made for the mountaintops.

A man was yelling now; it seemed as though the shots had been aimed at the girl, but Angus couldn't be too sure about that. She was out of range anyway. The man was furious, jumping up and down and shouting away in a foreign lingo. But then, mind you, even English was foreign to Angus. Now the firing had ceased, something had begun to swell up on the deck of the boat and take the shape of a seal. Ach, surely not! Then Angus realised it was one of those inflatable dinghies he had read about in *J D Mackay's Catalogue*. Yes, right enough, the man dropped it into the water and began to paddle it vigorously in the direction of the woman; but by this time she had managed to reach the shore.

She abandoned the boat in her hurry and scrambled up the rocks. God knows how, in high heels. Why on earth didn't she take them off and run in her bare feet? Angus couldn't help feeling sorry for her. He hoped the man would not catch up with her; then he saw her stop (out of the man's view). She seemed to bend down and remove her shoes, and looked as though she were trying to hide them under the bracken. After that she was off again at the double, climbing pretty high now, the man still after her. He was gaining on her too. So Angus thought it was time he had a hand in this intrigue – he started to stalk them both. He enjoyed himself fine, felt as though he were having a slight revenge on behalf of the perpetually hunted deer.

That lassie was going at a hell of a lick now that she had cast off her high heels. She had nearly reached the top of a very dangerous pinnacle when the man caught up with her. As he did so the woman turned and flashed a pistol in his face, but he threw her arm up before she had time to pull the trigger and in doing so disturbed her balance. She fell backwards letting out the most hair-raising yell Angus had ever heard. Down, down, down she went, bouncing off the boulders like a rubber ball.

Now, you would think that the man would have climbed down after her to see if she were still alive – but not him. The blighter started to run hell for leather down the hill; it looked as though he were making for the boats again. It was then that Angus came out into the full open; he would have to reach the girl himself to find out if she were still breathing, then get to the boats before the man would have time to lift anchor. He zigzagged like a snake in the long bracken, rising and stretching from rock to rock until he reached her at last and saw that she was indeed dead.

He started to put a prayer up for her and moved her fair hair from across her face. He felt choked with the pity of it, and numb, till a bullet whisked past his ear and reminded him of his own purpose and the peril in all this. So he roused himself; the only thing to do he thought was to beat the man to the dinghy, not give him the chance to get aboard the cruiser. He had his penknife with him so he would let the wind out of the inflatable dinghy and scuttle the other one, but first he must take a look at where the girl had so carefully hidden the shoes. He could still get to the boats before the man; the daft idiot was making down the most difficult side of the cliffs.

Angus kept crawling low, avoiding being seen or crackling the dry bracken – no one could be better at this hide-and-seek game than himself – many's the time he had played it with the deer. When he came up to the spot where the shoes were hidden he examined them critically; after all, he knew something about shoes – being a cobbler's son. He handled the delicate high heels curiously and was astonished to find they unscrewed, came right off, revealing some kind of mechanism on the inside; in the one a sort of camera, in the other a queer thing he had never seen before. He was so absorbed in his discovery that he didn't notice the man had crept up on him . . . the next thing he knew was the feel of hard steel between his shoulder blades and an English voice saying, 'Drop those shoes!'

'Certainly, sir!' said Angus as he dropped the shoes to the ground and in a trice flung his arms back around the man's neck and hurled him over his shoulder just as he would have done with the caber at the Isleornsay Games – after all hadn't he won the prize two years running? You should have seen the poor fellow rolling down the bealach, just like a log, and landing at the feet of old Moses, who had heard the shots and come hurrying out to investigate. So it was no trouble at all for Angus with the help of Moses and his dog Makarios to get the fellow trussed up like a cockerel, and drag him down to the side of the house where they made him fast to the wheel of the old cart. And it didn't take long either for Angus to cycle to the village on his bicycle to fetch the policeman. You should have seen his face – Big Archie thought he was lying and wouldn't believe a word of it – till Angus showed him the heels of the shoes which he had in his pocket.

Well, when they reached the house there was no sign of the man; only Angus's best gallaces lying on the ground beside the cartwheel, the ones he had used to tie him up with. It was not till they got inside the house that they found him sitting by the kitchen fire with a strupag (cup of tea) in his hand, guzzling away at scones and chatting to his mother and father, quite the thing!

'What the hell?' Angus said. 'Why did you let him loose?'

'Ach well, you see,' said Angus' father, 'the gentleman was only pursuing his duty. He is what you call a Special Agent, and the poor unfortunate woman was making off with highly confidential stuff that was hidden in the heels of her shoes, you understand?'

'What proof have you got of what you are saying?' said Big Archie, taking out his notebook.

Well, it took some weeks and a special investigation by detectives from Glasgow and Scotland Yard before they got to the bottom of the matter. It seems that the shoes that the girl was trying to hide contained vital information about our latest aircraft, and the man who had been following her all round Scotland was one of our own secret agents. The coroner's verdict on the woman's death was 'misadventure due to a climbing accident'. Nevertheless, Angus put a wee cairn of stones at the place where her body had lain – after all, she had been a dainty-looking lass.

And all that winter Angus and his father could hardly cope with the orders they got from the CID for stag-horn whistles and gillie shoes with tassels on them. . . . It was not till he felt the prod of his father's tackety boot on his backside that Angus woke up.

'What on earth do you think you are doing there, sleeping and dreaming all day long, and your mother waiting for you to bring the cows in for the milking!' bellowed his father. 'And you've still to do your homework . . . 'N ainm an àigh! Greas ort. Amadan!'* And they made their way back home along the edge of Loch Hourn to the little shooting lodge.

* 'N ainm an àigh! Greas ort. Amadan! – For heaven's sake, hurry up, you fool!

Pipe Dreams

If you're ever feeling depressed or seeking for a bit of real entertainment, you should take a run through to the auction sales at Oban. Not the cattle sales, the furniture sales; mind you, I'm not promising any great bargains, as all the big Sassenach dealers have found their way there now, and there's the ring, of course, but I'll not go into any details about that just now. For I've just got time to tell you a very strange story.

There was an elderly man and his wife, retired, living in a remote cottage not far from Loch Awe (sinister place that if ever there was one) and they had brought very little furniture with them from the last place they were in.

'Murdo,' his wife kept pestering, 'I wish to goodness you'd rouse yourself and take a wee run into Oban and see what's in the sales. Here, look at the *Oban Times*; there's one on Thursday (and she flung the paper into his lap). I'm pretty sure you could get a kitchen dresser or a chest o' drawers . . . half our stuff is still in tea chests since we came here, and I'm sick to death of it.'

So, partly to be out of her way (for she was an awful nagger) and partly to meet up with some of his cronies around the Oban bars, Murdo caught the bus on Thursday morning and arrived (after refreshing himself here and there) just as the sale was coming to an end. There had been dressers and chests of drawers aplenty, but they were all sold. The crowd had thinned out, and, but for the dealers and a few other people mostly consisting of Pakistani bus drivers looking for a bargain in double bed settees and Oban landladies beating them to it, there was nothing really left; nothing, that is, save an old seaman's chest well battered and with one brass handle missing.

'It would have to do, though,' said Murdo to himself, for he daren't go home without something; there would be hell to pay, and him not quite as steady on his feet as he might have been. So, as his hand went up he regained his balance and restarted the bidding: 'Two shillings and six pence,' he muttered shyly.

'Two and six I'm offered,' boomed the auctioneer, 'any advance on two and six pence . . . come along, chentlemen, this is a chenuine antique.'

'Aye, oot the Ark,' said one of the Glasgow dealers. 'Six shillings and it's no worth it.'

'Eight,' said Murdo, and he got a sharp dig in the ribs from his pal Angus.

'Are you daft, man? It's no good bidding in English. Try the Gaelic and he'll drop it to you like a scalded cat.'

'Is that right?' asked Murdo incredulously.

'Stop that talking or I'll clear the hall!' yelled the auctioneer. 'I need to get home to my haddocks even if you don't. I've a standing offer of ten shillings for the aforesaid magnificent keisht that you are seeing before your very eyes . . . you couldn't make the like of that today even if you tried. Alec, man, shove that girdle, the wellington boots and the two wally dugs* inside; we'll need to get home. There you are now,' he continued, 'there's a mystery chest for you. I'm offered ten shillings for a mystery chest . . . twelve and six . . . serteen shillings over there . . . It's going against you, sir,' he said pointing at Murdo, 'going at serteen shillings for the last time . . . going, going . . .'

* wally dugs – ornamental porcelain dogs displayed in pairs on mantelpieces

'N-òt!' shouted Murdo in the Gaelic, frantically waving a pound note.

"N-òt 's aon,'* replied the auctioneer, dropping his hammer with a mighty thud and smiling a respectful grin. 'To Mister Murdo Murchison, one pound sterling . . . uist e† . . . pay as you go out!'

And Murdo arrived home about midnight, with the chest tied on to the back of an army lorry that happened to be passing through to Taynuilt. In the morning his wife surveyed the new purchase, the blood pressure mounting in the back of her neck so that he thought she was in for another bad turn.

'In the name of God,' she shouted, 'in the name of the wee man, in the name of all . . .' But Murdo didn't wait for any more names to be called; he was away down to the turnip field till the storm would blow over.

Mind you, after a time the old chest didn't look all that bad sitting in the window with the caster oil plant on it. 'There's the rubbish that came out of it then,' his wife moaned, 'this rusty girdle's no good on earth to me, and you can feed the wellington boots to the cows if you like; God knows, they're well chewed already.'

'Aye,' but the wally dugs look grand on the mantelpiece,' ventured Murdo.

'Huh,' snorted his wife, 'and by the way, you'd better try to open the wee drawer that's in the blooming thing . . . it's stuck.' Murdo ceased chopping up his black twist tobacco and, raising the lid of the chest, he applied the knife gently to the stuck drawer – it was a kind of secret drawer that sprung out when you discovered the trick of it. Suddenly it popped out and there inside was a beautiful porcelain pipe, the picture of a

* 'N-òt 's aon – One pound only
† uist e – it's over

full-bosomed woman painted on the bulbous bowl and the curved stem was gilded in real gold.

Murdo was so enamoured with it that he didn't hear any more of his wife's scathing remarks. He made for his old leather armchair and kicking off his boots settled for a good long pull at the new pipe, and as he drew on it he began to feel sleepy. Everything was merging before his eyes, strange shapes were forming out of the smoke – people, men and women. There was the woman dressed in pink and mauve that was painted on the bowl of the pipe . . . and a man in red velvet knickerbockers. They sat down in the smoke clouds and seemed to make themselves quite comfortable, then they began to nod to him; they drew nearer and began to talk first about the weather, then about themselves, quite natural like; they asked him to join them sometime; and he said he would be glad to . . . 'I will, I will . . . you can be sure . . . I will . . .'

'You will what?' shouted his wife, shaking the daylights out of him. 'Don't just sit there dreaming and sucking away at that dirty old pipe – go on out and feed the hens!'

But Murdo hardly recognised his wife as she stood there shaking him; she seemed like a stranger. He felt embarrassed, but quickly he did as she bid him. Then, as the evening drew in, once more he sneaked back into his chair and lit up the pipe. It happened again much more vividly; these people were now real friendly, welcoming and they had a great céilidh that night . . . the lady sang for him his favourite songs and the man (called Phillip) was generosity itself with the drink . . . And this time when his real wife shook him again to give him a mug of hot milk he was real angry. She had never seen him like this before, and consequently showed him a good deal more respect.

Next day she had to go into Oban herself. She would buy

him a new semmit and drawers; he was badly needing them. And he on the other hand was glad to get the place to himself; lit up his pipe at the very first opportunity, it was all as it was before – almost like coming home they were so good to him. The woman was so soft and gentle, whispered that she had always loved him . . . half conscious Murdo replied that he thought, maybe . . . he was already married . . .

'And what of that?' said the man, 'you know you never really loved her. Why not get rid of her, it's easy.'

'How?' said Murdo.

'Why, kill her of course,' said the man.

And that same night when his wife got back, tired from shopping in Oban, Murdo upped and turned on her. 'Who asked you to buy me semmits and drawers? How dare you . . . such impertinence indeed! Get out of my house this instant, this is no place for the like of you! And, anyway, I have company coming to see me, real gentry, a chentleman of breeding and quality; a beautiful creature accompanying him whom I hope shortly to make my wife.'

'But I'm your wife,' blubbered his now terrified real wife, 'what on earth's come over you? If I've said anything or, or . . . oh, Murdo as sure as death I'm sorry, I meant no harm. I won't, I . . .'

'Get out of here you beesom!' he yelled, waving the poker at her and chasing her round the room, 'I never set eyes on you in my life before and neither do I want to . . . so, get out!' Down the croft he chased her and didn't turn till she had reached the main road.

She was in a proper lather when she at last reached a doctor. He had to give her a sedative, and he had to give more than a sedative to poor Murdo when he got to him. He was by now a very ill man. They had to get him into hospital straight away and pump out his stomach before they could get rid of all the poison. 'Heroin,' they said it was. It had been in the bowl of the pipe, you see, that he had never bothered to clean out; the pipe, which incidentally had brought about a miraculous change in his new 'beloved wife'. For her, the sun rose and shone on Murdo's fast balding head, and he could do no wrong. For little did he know that all she had ever wanted was a strong, fierce male capable of pelting her around . . . and, of course, a chest of drawers.

Tinker's Tale

There was a tinker once who liked to pitch his tent in or around Loch Fyne. He had not always been a tinker; there was a spell during World War I when he had been batman to a very scholarly legal gentleman serving in the Cameron High-landers. Roddy had a tremendous admiration for his parti-cular officer – 'a fine upstanding man, the Major, a man of quality' – he would lay down his life for him any day. And in fact they had experienced many hardships together. Shaving with snow, sleeping on burning sand, sheltering under hedges, chasing flies, finding booze and catching birds, with or without wings. Sleeping in the open was the least of the hardships for Roddy, him being born to it.

And now that the war was over Roddy found that he just couldn't take to living a civilian life, so he easily reverted to being a tinker again. The only thing, money was awful hard to come by; stealing a horse or a hen seemed more of a sin than it used to be. You had the law on you before you knew what hit you. The last time he went and got drunk he found himself up at Jack Simpson's farm trying to mount the grey mare – 'with every intention of stealing it' so they said – but Roddy couldn't remember a thing about it. He was still half asleep and 'not quite himself yet', so they dragged him rather unwillingly up before the fiscal.

Now it so happened that Roddy was a very good mimic and natural ventriloquist, without being aware of it, him being frequently 'under the influence' and nearly always 'not quite himself'. When they got him in the dock and managed to prop him up, the fiscal opened his mouth, about to say 'Raise your right hand,' etcetera; but it was Roddy's voice that came out of it: using the most complicated legal terms, he proceeded to charge himself and ask himself if he had anything more to say.

He then put his own case (very favourably, needless to say) in his normal if rather vulgar tinker fashion, then rapidly changed back to the polished and learned manner of the fiscal to pronounce judgement on himself. The poor fiscal was so astounded that he was stricken speechless.

It is hard to believe, I know, but Roddy had acquired a sound legal education in his sleep; his subconscious mind had absorbed every word from the many books his officer read aloud during the long months in which they had shared a life together under the same canvas. Well, Roddy got his freedom, but was wise enough to let the grey mare go. You can't push your luck too far – every Romany knows that.

Pidgeon's Eggs

Her name was Conchita Manuela Ornandez Enamorado. They called her Chi-chi for short. She lived in a large house in the Midlands and had eleven brothers. They were all under thirty and studied medicine, dentistry, engineering and politics at Manchester and Liverpool universities. Each and every one of them played a musical instrument divinely. Chi-chi made coffee for them every evening in an enormous fish kettle, gurgling away on the stove. They used the basement of the old house as their communal study and Chi-chi dished out their coffee into large mugs with a soup ladle that normally hung on the wall.

Chi-chi loved her brothers and cared for them diligently. When examinations were pending and work continued into the night she would cook up a pot of potatoes, mash them with butter smooth like paste, and serve it like a white mountain on a large ashet wiped with garlic, handing round individual bowls of milk to go with it.* Then she set up her easel and started to paint; nothing would induce her to go to bed before they did. Their parents were religious, and very strict. Señor Enamorado had interests in the Canary Islands and Cuba; he was now a retired consul and occupied himself mainly with the export and import trade. Señora Enamorado, his wife, was a charming hostess and taught her one and only daughter all the graces; to play the piano, speak French and

* Threepenny bits were hidden inside the potatoes and this dish found its way to the Highlands known as 'buntàta bruain'.

73

German, do Italian quilting and petit point, pour tea from a Queen Anne teapot and make introductions – to say nothing of art. Chi-chi loved art best of all, and that's how I met her.

We both turned up at the same art classes held by a Madame Crighton; about thirty pupils, boys and girls mixed. Chi-chi would arrive three days a week, escorted by an elderly maid; she never went anywhere without a chaperone, according to Spanish custom. Eventually, I was invited to her home, respecting with her all its traditions, quickly absorbing the atmosphere.

You entered a sunlit hall with red and gold damask wallpaper. At the foot of the stairs you curtsied and crossed yourself to a shrine of the Virgin Mary, all lit up and surrounded with fresh flowers. The house was never without music, upstairs in the drawing room. The Señora would greet you with outstretched hand and invite you to choose, from a five-tiered cake stand, some delicate gateau or sweet. Over the mantelpiece there was a portrait of a British lieutenant in uniform and medals; right in the middle of his forehead was a mark like a bullet wound. This portrait fascinated me and I longed to hear the story of how he got the wound and who he was. Chi-chi was evasive when I asked her, and it seemed as though she really didn't know.

'It was Mama's,' she said. 'She just likes it. He's no relation.' But it was not the sort of house to hang the portrait of an unknown soldier, whatever the rank. I was mystified, till some three years later I went to do some painting in the Channel Isles.

As the steamer ploughed its way towards Guernsey, I felt cold and wet, and went below for some coffee; the saloon was crowded with holidaymakers. I managed to squeeze myself in at a table with a very large sullen-looking man sitting opposite me. When he raised his head I knew who he was, instantly. I'd seen him before many times. The thick hair was slightly grey, but the face was young and handsome as ever, the mark on the forehead unmistakable.

It was he who spoke first, 'Rotten weather. The channel is shallow hereabouts, makes her roll a bit. You a good sailor?'

'Yes,' I ventured. 'Please don't think me forward or fatuous, if I say haven't I seen you somewhere before?'

'Unfortunately, no. It has never been my good fortune to see you, mademoiselle.'

He had such charm of manner I felt I could talk to him freely, as though I had known him for a long time. 'I have seen your portrait, in the house of Señora Enamorado. It must be you? It's exactly like you.'

He looked completely blank. 'It might well be,' he said. 'How long ago is it since you saw it?'

'When I was fourteen.'

He laughed. 'You are little more than that now? I know . . . I know I must be serious. Do you see this wound in my forehead, Mademoiselle? I got it in exchange for my memory. I know nothing of the friends you speak about, and I am not aware of ever having had my portrait painted – amnesia I think you call it.'

'Oh, I'm terribly sorry, I didn't want to dig things up. Your past I mean, I would never . . .' I was at a loss for words.

'I'm glad you did. I was longing for someone to talk to, and I must hear more about my portrait. What is your destination, mademoiselle?'

'Why, Guernsey. I intend to stay there for a short time to capture the Victor Hugo atmosphere on canvas.'

'Then tomorrow, perhaps, we could have lunch together. I would be honoured to carry your equipment, and we could visit the haunts of the revered poet.'

'Well, thank you, I will. Your name is . . .'

'Ralph Pidgeon.'

'Lieutenant Pidgeon? In the portrait you were wearing uniform.'

'I know nothing of that. A pigeon was the first living thing I saw when I came out of the anaesthetic, and Ralph was the name of the doctor.'

The following day there was a wind that tried to lift me off my feet; I had arranged to meet Ralph Pidgeon at the pier. He had given me the telephone number of the friends he stayed with; somewhere in the centre of the Island. I decided to call him (on account of the weather) and postpone our date, when my room phone rang: 'Gentleman to see you, miss, he is waiting down below.'

'I didn't want the high winds to whisk you off like a little piece of thistledown,' Ralph said when I greeted him. 'There's a place I know that can give us oysters and ormurs baked in wine; they even serve hot toddy from a toddy bowl. I have borrowed an old jalopy. So let's go!' After lunch we motored around to find the haunts of Victor Hugo, and eventually came on a house washed by wind and rain, bleached to a pinkish shade that I ached to paint. Standing in its dining room, our exuberant spirits were slowly being smothered. It was as though the sinking sands the exile loved to write about were enveloping us. Then a falling shaft of light led us out of the room, and we made our way up to the tower. There we could breathe. We looked out over the miles of sand and sea, over towards France. 'How he must have suffered in his exile,' I said.

Ralph laid his hand gently on my shoulder. 'I know all there is to know about that,' he said, 'to be a dropped link from a human chain – a human chain that is mended again and pulling its weight without you.'

'Then, you do remember some of your past?'

'Only the bad bits, the sound of firing and trying to wipe the mixture of sand and blood off my face. It's as though one were sifting something through a sieve, only the lumpy bits remain: "With you I'll breathe the air which ye expire, and, smiling, hide my melancholy lyre when it is wet with tears."'

'Victor Hugo,' we both said simultaneously. 'Couldn't you let me help you?' I felt I must do something, my heart ached so for him.

'You are helping, my little piece of thistledown, by bringing a seed which might take root in my memory. Keep talking to me, tell me all about your friends.'

'All right. Well, there's a Chi-chi, her real name Conchita Manuella Ornandez Enamorado . . . rather a mouthful.'

'Wait, please, excuse me,' he interrupted, 'don't go on for a moment. There are too many lumps in the sieve.' He sat down abruptly on a deck chair with a green canvas cover over it; the reflection of light made his face look green, also, as though he were going to be sick, or faint.

I knelt quickly down beside him and took both of his hands in mine: 'Are you all right, can I get you anything?'

'No, no, please no. Conchita, Conchita,' he said in a breathless sort of way, then, in a perfectly normal voice, 'it's all coming back to me. Conchita was the name of my wife; she is dead now. It was in 1938, I was a volunteer Spanish Royalist. I was really in the British army, but relinquished all that when war broke out in Spain.'

'Begin at the beginning,' I said. The colour was returning to his face again; he had got over the first shock of remembering.

'All right. I was born in Devon; my father was an artist, Theodore Rigby. I remember clearly now, my mother died when I was born. I joined the Officers' Training Corps at school and, as I couldn't paint, I decided to remain a soldier; eventually I became a lieutenant. In the summer holidays my father would take me to Spain. He had an obsession for painting bulls and bullfights.

'One day we had got too close to a young bullock and it gored me in the forehead. While I was convalescing father painted my portrait (he had done so many times); at the same time he had been commissioned to do a painting of a beautiful young Spanish girl called Conchita Ornandez. She came every afternoon for a sitting and I fell madly in love with her. My father encouraged me in this; he agreed that she was quite the most beautiful girl we had ever seen and what a model, still and composed like a madonna. I lost no time in making a formal proposal of marriage, and was flatly refused, not by her, of course; she loved me equally as I loved her. Nevertheless, her parents would not hear of her marrying a non-Catholic and her pious married sister Lela Enamorado, preparing her first three sons for confirmation, nearly had convulsions when she heard of it.

'There was only one thing to do – elope. So, after elaborate planning we did this, and stayed with my father till we could find a priest who would marry us. Well, you know how it is. The whole business took weeks and even months. Conchita tried to create a little home for us in my father's studio, and he would come each day to work bringing with him food and wine . . . the war was well underway by now, and our marriage problems didn't interest anyone. It was survival of the fittest, nothing else mattered . . . Then it came to us on a sunny February afternoon – a bomb hit the glass roof of the studio, my father was killed outright, and I was carried off in an ambulance, badly wounded and unconscious. Poor Conchita flew to the mercy of her sister Lela Enamorado – she took her in reluctantly, and when our child was born she adopted it, a little girl.

'It was nearly a year before they let me out of hospital, still suffering from spasmodic amnesia and I tried in vain to find my Conchita. Eventually I learned that, after the child was born, she had joined a high order of nuns, and, on Lela's advice, had taken the veil, wearing the sin of our love heavily on her sad little shoulders. A few months later she died, and the Enamorados had taken the child to England.

'This girl, Chi-chi, must be mine; my little girl that I have never seen.' He leaned his head in his hands, and was silent for a long time. Then, abruptly, he said, 'Look, can we meet again tomorrow? I feel ill and tired. I must return to the farm where I stay. I intend to charter a small boat to go to the Island of Jethou tomorrow morning; will you join me, mademoiselle?'

'Why, of course.' So, we set out from La Vallete, where a small motorboat had been fuelled and made ready for us. I asked Ralph what his mission was.

'Oh, of course, you don't know. I am an ornithologist. How should you? I watch birds and look for rare eggs, that sort of thing. They interest me for my collection.'

'Oh, well, I've brought my paints along.'

'All aboard then, hand me your stuff, and we're off!'

It was a sunny, mystic sort of day, veiled in a sea haar, the monophonic rhythm of the engine lulled me, till we were quite near Jethou. Suddenly, we heard a couple of shots ring out in the distance. They seemed to be coming from an old building near the shore. We quickly made fast to another boat, moored alongside a small jetty and clambered ashore, in time to see a man running out from the building, hotly pursued by two others. They chased him far into the distance till their shapes became charcoal miniatures fading in the mist.

'What do you think it is?' I said.

Ralph stood watching with a sort of sinister grin on his face. 'I don't know. Let's go and find out.'

So we made our way along a shore track towards the house. It was old and dilapidated, and hadn't been lived in for some time. Walls, barns and outhouses were all overgrown with ivy wisteria and deadly nightshade. Ralph began to look eagerly around. He seemed excited and feverish today. I felt there was something on his mind.

So I set up my easel and started to paint, while he ferreted about relentlessly. Then he called me urgently: 'I've found six beauties, come and help me!' I dropped my brushes and joined him. Out of a large bird's nest hidden behind a clump of wisteria he gently lifted the eggs. 'Don't worry,' he said, 'I will replace them with ordinary ones. Hold this box.' It was a cardboard box marked 'Eggs – Fragile'. He covered each one with cotton wool and tied them securely. He would not let me touch them. I had seldom seen such beauties; all speckled and very large.

'They look bigger than usual,' I said.

'Of course, they are very rare indeed. But I have disturbed your painting.' After I had resumed work he sat down beside me on the grass.

Gradually, I began to feel strangely tense. Some of his personality was creeping into my work, a restless furtiveness. I found myself painting little fences where they didn't exist, trying to create a barrier . . . the man was twice my age, why should I feel like this? He put his hand on my knee and, although I resented it, I couldn't move it away. I was aware of his making demands on my imagination, sort of refuelling at my expense. I determined that I would not spend more time alone with him than was strictly necessary. Suddenly I found myself saying, 'I must go home next week.' To my surprise he did not demur.

'Splendid,' he said. 'You can take the eggs with you. In your care they will be less likely to get broken, and I shall have a valid excuse for calling on you to collect them.'

'Oh dear.'

That night I wrote to Chi-chi, the usual scribble; fine

weather, good time, interesting subjects to paint, and an intriguing distraction, a man old enough to be my father. I didn't say that he in fact claimed to be her father; this I would never say. Chi-chi was far too happy and contented as she was. The Señor and Señora obviously loved her dearly – however, there would be no harm in letting them meet sometime. I told her that he had given me a box of rare seabird's eggs to bring back for him, and that he would collect them at my flat when I returned on Tuesday, with luck, and that was all.

At the weekend the weather broke. There was torrential rain. I stayed in bed and read the papers. Reluctantly, I hoped that Ralph would ring me. The papers were full of the usual weekend drivel, including an account of the arrest of a man on Jethou who was taken to Guernsey for questioning. Twenty minutes after leaving the police station he was found dead, shot through the head. I wondered about it sleepily, then turned the page to the women's column . . . shift dresses were in again. I was disappointed that Ralph didn't come to see me off on the steamer, and wondered what had happened to him. Well, after all, I hadn't given him much encouragement. I had only cruelly opened up old wounds. No wonder he avoided me.

When my boat train got into London, I was surprised to hear my name being called from the loudspeakers: would I go to the station master's office, there was a message for me. I laughed, thought it would be Ralph. Maybe he had flown over? But no, it was Señor Enamorado who was waiting for me, with two plain-clothed detectives. They seized my egg box marked 'Eggs – Fragile', while I protested loudly.

'It's all right,' Enamorado said, 'they must open it.'

When they saw the speckled eggs all three started to laugh. 'Real plastic plovers' eggs,' the Scots one said. 'He's a genius, Ah hand it to him. What did he say his name was this time, Miss?'

'Do you mean Ralph Pidgeon? He's a gentleman and an officer.'

'He's a conman and a smuggler you mean,' Enamorado said, taking my arm gently. 'Your letter to Chi-chi aroused my suspicions. I contacted the police immediately. He is an old hand at the game. I had trouble with him when I first started in the export trade. We found heroin aboard one of our ships and I had him jailed for fifteen years. Now he's out and at it again. They found his contact man in Jethou. The police let him go as they had insufficient evidence. That night Pidgeon shot him. He's a dangerous man and we have no time to lose. You give your key to these two gentlemen and they will go to your flat in advance and let themselves in – you come and have a cup of coffee with me in the station hotel, and carry the egg box quite openly. You are sure to be watched and even followed. Then I will escort you home. The detectives will let us in and hide themselves till whoever comes to collect the eggs arrives. I will then leave the flat and hide myself in some convenience, or I should say, convenient place, until the action starts. I am sorry you got yourself involved in all this, a chaperone is so essential. On the other hand you are helping to rid your country of one of its vilest criminals.'

We arrived at the flat and the detectives hid as planned. I put the eggs on a table in the middle of the room, removed my hat and boiled the kettle. Señor Enamorado had promised to stay very close.

I just had time to turn the kettle off when the doorbell rang – it was Ralph looking very smart and beaming: 'My dear, I missed you so much. I tried to stay away, but couldn't. I was desolate and I took the first plane over. I wondered if we could have lunch together tomorrow? I must take the eggs to the taxidermist in the morning and collect you here after-wards, perhaps? If you give them to me now I shall run away and let you rest after your horrid sail. Why you don't fly I can't imagine!' He reached for the eggs; the detectives simultaneously leapt in his direction.

Before they could touch him, he had the box of eggs in one hand and a gun in the other . . . slowly, he moved backwards to the door, keeping us covered. Then, noiselessly and mercifully, the door opened and Enamorado grabbed both his arms, and relieved him of his gun. The detectives did the rest.

'How do you like your eggs boiled, mister?' the Scotsman asked. Ralph Pidgeon looked beyond him at me, with a cold hard look.

'You are a most convincing liar,' I said.

'He is more than that,' said the Scotsman. 'He's a regular wee James Bond, but he's aye on the wrong side, and let's face it, at his age he's past it.'

Riley the Poltergeist

The front door opened, causing an unholy blast of wind that made the back door fly wide open at the same time, and the long galvanised tin bath hanging on the scullery wall bashed out its clanging ovation to my husband Kazik, a penniless Pole whom I had married at the end of the war.*

'Shut that door!' (we must have coined the phrase), and I reached to embrace the tall handsome man that had made my life worthwhile. The magic and the happiness of living on the Eyebrow Hill in this tiny, 400-year-old gate lodge, with its octagonal roof and three chimneys, cannot be described.

The estate had once belonged to members of our oldest Scottish aristocracy, the Hamiltons. The charming old place, known as The Peel, was situated in the green belt between Glasgow and Lanarkshire, owned by an antique dealer who had filled the house with unbelievable treasures. He was friendly to us, admiring the Poles, and listening (his mouth wide open) to Kazik's stories of the Resistance Movement in which he had been so involved. He also appreciated my own interest – not so much in the antiques trade, but the stuff itself. I had what they call a nose for it, a sort of sixth sense; not surprising, since I came from the Isle of Skye, and had no doubt inherited the psychic instincts of my Highland forbears and the name, Rebecca, from my grandmother.

I had been getting waves of intuition more strongly in the

* This story is true.

last few days, together with feelings of guilt. You see, I was the oldest of my family and my mother and father had died some years back now and were buried in Skye without a headstone.

We had got a foundry on the Clyde to make a bronze plaque for each of them, but kept passing the buck as to who should have the honour of setting them in a suitable gravestone. My sister in New Zealand was too inaccessible, and my other sister – recently married – was constantly occupied with raising her family; and we, let's face it, were far too poor to travel so far, having no means of transport and very little so-called holiday time, for Kazik was working as a scientific engineer on all sorts of new inventions for Kelvin Hughes (Hoover Company Limited).

Most of these inventions matured in his mind as he lay in the long, tin bath, while I reheated the water from an immense, heavy antique iron kettle that my Highland granny had once owned, and took care in the dim light of an oil lamp not to endanger any future progeny that we might have by pouring the boiling water, or even dropping the kettle accidentally. So, on these balmy, gentle, idyllic evenings we would make our plans for the future, anticipating all kinds of miraculous changes of fortune when our boat would at last come home.

One morning in spring, gathering an armful of wild daffodils on my way back from the bus stop, having had to run after Kazik who had forgotten his briefcase, I met our landlord coming down the drive. 'For goodness sake,' he said, 'when are you two going to get yourselves a car?'

'Can't afford it, Dicky, old boy!' I replied.

'Well, look!' he said. 'It so happens I had to take an old Riley against a bad debt. I could let you have it for dirt cheap – say, five hundred pounds? It's in perfect nick. The engine needs adjusting a little, that's all, and Kazik could do that in half an hour.'

'We haven't got five shillings, let alone five hundred pounds, so don't talk daft!'

'Yes, I know,' he said, 'but you have got a bow-fronted, Dutch mahogany chest of drawers. Maybe we could do a deal?'

And vividly, immediately, I could see what all my psychic, guilt-ridden, intuitive feelings had been about – a car, a trip to Skye (Kazik and the spring holiday due) and so, over a cup of coffee Dicky and I pitted our wits against each other. The chest of drawers was a magnificent piece; I knew it as well as he. I had bought it at a house sale near Culross. It had belonged to a family called Bruce and was reputed to have come from the old Palace, now protected by the National Trust for Scotland.

I had wondered why there were so few bidding against me at the sale. It was dropped to me for about five pounds, all I had at the time, but when I came to remove it I found out why – it was riddled with woodworm. I was so upset I tackled the auctioneer about it and I never forgot his reply: 'Your eyes are your money, lady!' And he was right, of course, there had been two days to view the stuff. Taking Kazik's handkerchief to dry my tears that night I asked him to forgive me.

'Don't cry, Ronishau,' he said. 'It is easy, it is nossing. I know I can kill dhis worm in two days. It is a wonderful buy, do you realise . . .'; and he began to mull over the workmanship of the superbly designed chest. The heavy, brass handles, original and hand-wrought, the graceful, flowing shapes of the drawers – a very handsome, very early Dutch piece of furniture; he got to work immediately on concocting a potion that would kill off the worm. Taking my soup ladle, a junior saw and so on he went out and found an ancient rotting tree. The inside was hollow, and a thick mushy liquid had accumulated there. He extracted it into a pail, then added drops of various chemicals that he had in a shed at the side of the house for his numerous experiments, and, sure enough, it worked. The chest was cured entirely of the woodworm. Of course, nothing would induce me to sell it at any price, but this was different; this swap for a car was the answer to my prayers.

It took Kazik two days to get the engine running to his satisfaction, although he would rather have spent much more time on it; I would not let him I was so eager to be off. So, with plenty of jerseys and a good pile of provisions, including some tinned octopus paws which Kazik maintained were necessary for vitamins and sustenance, we tried to find Anniesland Cross and the Great North Road. I was no help whatsoever. My sense of direction simply doesn't exist. So, with my little Yorkshire terrier Petrushka on my knee, I placed all my fate in my husband's hands, never having seen him drive before. It astonished me how good he was at it, but then he was good at everything.

That night we camped outside Fort William. It was our first experience of sleeping rough, and a test for a great deal more to come. I had planned to camp at the side of the Strollamus Graveyard in Skye, rather than stay with relatives or friends. We had so very little time, and it would not be easy to collect suitable, and I'd hoped, lovely, stones from the shore, and cement them in artistically round the bronze plaques.

On Skye, at first, the weather was favourable, and we got to work with great enthusiasm. I made a Celtic cross with sand and cement, facing it with shells, and Kazik was making a wonderful job of the stone into which the cross and the plaque would be set. And then it came – the rain – in torrents. We wrapped ourselves in the hemp sacks we transported the cement in, built huge fires, heating tea and soup on a primus. Each morning Doctor Neil MacLeod would sail in with his boat with a string of fish, taught us how to cook them on the wood and peat fire. The tinkers also lost their shyness. Kazik's cigarettes were strong and much to their liking, so much so that in appreciation the old head of the family, a real Romany (his wit and appearance not unlike that of Peter Ustinov) generously assured us that he would not allow any of his children, his wife, his mother-in-law or his sister-in-law either, to pee or empty their slops, or in any way contaminate the river upstream from us. That was a relief!

And so, with our time more than run out, everything we possessed sogging wet, and only the knowledge that we had done a good job and got to know strange and beautiful people we might never otherwise have met, we packed and prepared to leave. Because of the constant rain, Kazik had kept a little lamp under the car to prevent her being water-logged, but when we came to start her up there simply wasn't a hope – it was Sunday and no possible way of finding a garage or mechanic that could help. What to do? 'There is only one thing,' said Kazik, 'ether!'

'Ether!' says I, 'where the hell can we get that?'

'The hospital, of course. You can walk that far; I tink it is no use for me to go, a foreigner with such a request, and me not even sick!'

So, squelching along in the driving rain I made it to the hospital and asked to see the matron. They immediately complied as I looked like a casualty washed in from the sea.

'Ether!' said she, stiffening like a pillar of salt. 'Certainly not! The very idea . . . for a car! In the name of the wee man!'* And then, 'What did you say your name was?'

'Rhona Rauszer, but my maiden name was MacLeod, nighean Mairianna Beathag,'† I explained in Gaelic – and you should have seen the change!

* In the name of the wee man – May Saint Maolrubha (patron of south Skye) bless us!
† nighean Mairianna Beathag – the daughter of Mairianna, the daughter of Rebecca

'Oh, sit down, dear, why didn't you say? I knew your mother well, dear . . . and you're so wet . . . wait till I ring for a cup of tea.' Needless to say I got the ether and a wee drop of alcohol besides (for medicinal purposes only, you understand)!

Now, you might be wondering why we called the car 'the Poltergeist' in the first place. Well, it all happened from now on. On our way back we had crossed the ferry, seen off by a bunch of my relatives, and were well on our way and exceedingly tired – and so, it seems, was the car. She suddenly heaved up, crashed over the concrete barriers on the sharp turn of the MacAlasdair Brae and down we went into a steep gorge. Petrushka was flung through the windscreen, mercifully unhurt. I fell out through the door which went hurling down into the river and Kazik was unhurt also – but 'Riley the Poltergeist' was a complete write-off. We struggled up to the road again and Kazik dabbed at a cut on my forehead. Cars passed us by the dozen, we were too weak and shattered to make much of an effort to stop any of them.

Then, a magnificent Rolls-Royce stopped; the chauffeur in grey livery got out and said most formally that his master was concerned for our plight and wondered if he could be of any help.

'Well, I have a cousin Rebecca Kennedy who has the Dalmally Hotel,' I said. 'If you could tell her to contact the AA.'

The chauffeur said they weren't going near Dalmally, however the boss said, 'Oh, but we are!' and left us two bottles of Guinness and some lobster sandwiches, and off they went. I never got his name or number, and to this day I'm not sure if he was real.

My old Auntie Teeny wasn't all that sure if he was real either, when he turned up at the hotel to tell of the accident.

With a slow, incredulous expression on her face she took in the situation – not before removing her spectacles from her nose to let the tears flow more freely (Auntie Teeny was never one to hold back her emotions).

'I knew it, I knew it,' she said. 'It came to me last night. I was wakened up in the middle of the night at three in the morning, or maybe it was four . . .'

'Yes, yes . . .' said the gentleman, 'we must hurry. Where is your daughter Rebecca?'

'That's it!' interrupted my aunt. 'That's what he said . . . my husband . . . he's dead a long while now, but he appeared suddenly in the flesh from behind the red plush curtains in my bedroom and shook his fist at me. "See to it!" he said, and he sounded angry. "See to it, woman, that the two Rebeccas meet . . . the two Rebeccas must meet!" . . . and then he disappeared like a puff of smoke . . . and he was a big man, a fine man.' Then she began to cry again copiously.

The gentleman offered his handkerchief and tried to calm her down. 'Tell me,' he said gently, 'where is your daughter Rebecca? I must know if I am to contact her for you, and them . . .'

'Well, they went over to Inveraray to get the hotel ready for the season. 'Sann aig Dhia a tha fios,' she blabbered in Gaelic (God knows when they will return).

The gentleman turned on his heel. 'At the double, Fred, we make for Inveraray. Now!'

'But, sir!' objected the chauffeur.

'No buts, get started!' And they drove all the way to Inveraray, where they found my cousin Rebecca. Her husband Jackie got the Jaguar out and they came immediately to our rescue, leaving the Poltergeist to the AA and staying the night with us at Dalmally.

We all had a party on the upstairs landing that night,

squatting in a circle in an assortment of Jackie's pyjamas (our luggage was somewhere in the MacAlasdair River) while Auntie Teeny, white-faced, her black hair sleekly drawn on either side of her face, her black chemise emphasising the whiteness of her arms and gesticulating with her long, thin hands, recounted the events of the night before.

'*The two Rebeccas must meet!*' he'd said, and Riley the Poltergeist had seen to it that we did!

Through time, a remote Highland garage sent us a cheque for thirty pounds for scrap and Kazik made me a very nice built-in chest of drawers out of some tea boxes. Bless him! (And we never saw the strange Samaritan or the Poltergeist again.)

The Golden-haired Maiden

In the depths of the pine forest that grows around the slopes of the great fierce, challenging mountains that surround Loch Carron, there was a little wooden hut where a widow woman lived alone save for her blind niece (some say she'd got the niece from the mountain fairies, but that is as maybe). Now, as you can well imagine, it was not too easy for the widow to fend for herself and her niece with no man around to care for them; she would wander for miles collecting the wool that the sheep left hanging on fences and dykes and weave it and knit it for jumpers. She taught her blind niece, whose name was Dornie, after the place, her being without parents and of no known origin, you understand; well, she taught her to knit beautifully and weave as well. But still, it wasn't easy to find a market for their work with them being so isolated; they were very poor indeed and often hungry. Dornie was seventeen, a rare beauty with hair of corn gold; and her eyes, though blind, were as deep, dark and bewitching as the peat bogs. She was, however, needing to start wearing shoes, maybe ribbons and the like to catch the eye of some young lad. But the widow was not too worried. She knew that Dornie would get a man some day; the banshee had told her so, many times, when she went to the tree for counsel – the magic tree that grew just outside in front of the hut.

Now, this particular tree at one time or another had been struck by lightning and stripped of all its bark; the shock had turned it white, given it a sort of power. It became a medium between mortals and the wee fey folk. Sometimes music would vibrate along its branches, from its hollow trunk tunes emerged, played better than on any chanter. Dornie's aunt discovered the powers of this tree through being very superstitious. When her hand itched she would rub it against the wood: 'Rub it on wood and it's sure to be good,' she'd say. She would make a wish remembering to use only the left hand: 'Left for love and right for spite.'

Well, one day when she was busy at this caper, a little old banshee appeared and asked her what it was she was wishing for.

'For sufficient gold to buy some food,' said Dornie's aunt.

'Shame on you, woman,' said the banshee. 'Are you so blind that you can't see gold before your very eyes?' Dornie's aunt looked all round, but could see no gold. Her eyes could see nothing gold at all until they caught a glimpse of Dornie's hair as she stood by the peat stack with her back to the setting sun – all around her the glowing light filtered through her hair.

'Go and comb your niece's hair,' said the banshee, 'comb it with love and care, and use a comb, mind, don't go near it with scissors or shears or you will never get your wish from me!' The widow did as she was bid; drawing a milking stool close to her niece she sat and with loving care took the golden locks in her hands. She combed and combed, and with every stroke fine golden strands of hair would come away with the comb; she was far too sentimental to throw them away.

And that same evening as she passed the magic tree the voice of the banshee said, 'Tomorrow morning take the combings of your niece's hair and roll them tightly in the palm of your left hand; then walk as far as Dingwall. When you get there sell the hair to the merchants.'

'But . . . but listen,' the widow started to say.

'Ah, ah, no buts,' said the banshee. 'Just get on your way at break of dawn, and don't look inside the palm of your hand until you get there.'

Next day the widow set off at break of dawn, right enough. When she at last reached Dingwall torn and bedraggled through taking short mountain tracks, she made for the nearest jewel merchants. Then and only then she opened her fist to sell him the hair. But to her surprise it was not hair . . . it had gone solid in her sweaty hand and was now a sizeable lump of gold! The merchant willingly gave her several sovereigns for it; she bought a dress and shoes for her niece and ribbons to put in her hair. When she got home she dressed her up in them like a fairy princess.

The widow made many trips to Dingwall after that but was always careful not to be too greedy or answer too many questions. Even then there were some that got wind of her activities, suspecting there was gold (in them there hills), went prospecting round her hut. They dug up the ground here, there and everywhere but they found nothing and eventually got fed up, went off home. Not long after that there was a young, handsome, sporting gentleman passing through the forest; he tripped and fell into one of the potholes the prospectors had made.

Although his injuries were not very grave you could hear his hollering echoing for miles up the mountain. The widow rushed to his aid, but to raise him up was beyond her strength. She called to her niece, instructing her to put her arm around him and heave.

This the girl did willingly, saying, 'My, my, but isn't he a smasher . . . look at the cut of his doublet!'

The widow was at first astonished to find that her blind niece could see: 'Sin agad e,' she said (in the Gaelic, that's it). She clapped her chubby arms across her bosoms, did a wee jump for the joy of it as she remembered the words the tree banshee had been saying to her:

> When a handsome young MacKinnon
> Comes hunting the wild boar
> The blindness will fall away from the girl
> The minute she puts her arms around him!

Spitting Image

The strong wind blowing up from the sea was driving her on; it was helpful as she was lumbering a rather heavy suitcase that kept swinging against her legs and holding her back. It contained all her worldly goods, put together by the Women's Guild. For Effie Mathieson was a sixteen-year-old orphan left in the care of the parish. Her father, a fisherman, had drowned at sea, and her mother had died of a broken heart. Thereafter, she was sent to an aunt who virtually brought her up, but just last year the very elderly aunt had taken a coronary and died. The little money they had was left to Effie Mathieson. Not much or enough to keep her in luxury for the rest of her days – she would have to find a job.

And the ladies of the Guild had got together in the manse to discuss in what way they could help this child. The minister was very friendly and very kind, but he quickly made his escape – for to be landed with some ten or fifteen women on a stormy afternoon all drinking tea and discussing what to do with a little sixteen-year-old girl, he didn't feel he could contribute much to the conversation. Off he went, while the ladies assembled round the edge of the wall waiting for their hostess, the minister's wife, to hand them over the plates of goodies; everything you could imagine – pancakes with cream and jam on, oatcakes with crowdie, fairy cakes, cream cakes, all there, set out on a central table with the best china and the best cloth – hand-embroidered as the lady of the house said, 'by the Marie Curie Society,' or some society that had got together to collect funds for that good cause. Each and all of the ladies in turn made a remark on the beauty of the cloth, the handwork of the stitching, the colouring and the lace, etcetera, etcetera, which was ironical really, because at least two of them were stone blind and couldn't see, but they still made the remarks, just the same.

After two hours of argy-bargy they agreed the best thing for the girl was to send her up the river to work with old Mrs McConnachie. She was getting very old and had bad arthritis, and at least the girl would help to bring in the coal and do some of the heavy chores. Mrs McConnachie had been housekeeper for many years now to a cranky old doctor of science, who had arrived on the island, oh, some twenty years ago and was a bit of a conundrum. Nobody got to know him, he didn't socialise, he didn't move with the people at all, kept himself mainly in his study. They said he was a boormaister.

A couple of the younger ladies of the Guild giggled behind their handkerchiefs, thought it was really tempting fate in a way, to send such a very pretty young girl up there to work for the old duffer: 'There might be a kick in him yet!' they whispered to each other.

So, her future planned out for her, Effie trundled up the hill high above sea level. Then she turned round to gaze at the village she was leaving behind. She was not sorry, although she was a bit frightened about what lay before her. With her head down, her new boots crunching the snow at the edges of the road, for it was winter, she continued on until she reached the sinister valley that lay up in the heart of the mountains. There were no houses about, they'd all gone long ago.

Her father had told her, 'Once upon a time, a long time ago there had been many houses up in that valley, about six, and a church, graveyard and manse. The whole lot, except for the old manse had been swept away in a terrible storm, hurricane almost, when the river had burst its banks, swollen right up and taken in its path all the houses, sucked the graveyard, all the gravestones out of the ground and swept them all down the river until they reached the bay below. And for many years,' her father had said, 'if you walked along the tide line you could still find skulls, human skulls, and the odd coffin battered to bits.' Effie didn't know whether to believe him or not, because he was very good at telling stories.

But now, as she made her way along in this dreary, eerie place she began to think it must all have been true. And the funny little circular mounds, now covered in snow, resembled whipped cream walnuts for all the world. They belonged to the Ice Age, when the snows melted and left them standing, with their circles like corkscrews all round them. They were very magical, of course. And across the river she could see the old manse still standing, two or three hundred years old at least. That was where she had to go, her destination. Taking her courage in both hands she crossed the rickety bridge.

The garden of the old manse went down nearly to the river, in fact, the privet hedge was in the river. The house itself was quite large and completely overgrown with Virginia creeper, crimson red, looking like blood had been spilt all over it. She began to be very frightened. There was a large black cat sitting on the front doorstep – Effie was frightened of cats. It snarled at her; she was frightened to go up the steps and ring the bell, stood there shivering with the old suitcase in her hand. It had belonged to her father, was made of a sort of green canvas and had the name of a ship printed in black on the edge. In it were all the things she'd gathered that belonged to her – mighty little: two skirts, two jumpers, two pairs of pants, two vests, a new pair of boots the schoolmistress had given her and the most precious thing she possessed in all the world – her little rag book with illustrations painted in it –

Humpty Dumpty, Little Bo Peep, the Cow that jumped over the Moon and, of course, Little Red Riding Hood. She saw herself now just like Little Red Riding Hood; when she got inside the house would she find a big hairy wolf, or what?

Then she saw a face at the window; shortly after that the door was opened. The cat was kicked down the steps and an enormous lady, her hair piled up on the top of her head with a large bun on top of that said, 'Oh well, you must be Effie Mathieson.' And this was of course Mrs McConnachie. There was no mistaking her. Effie thought she was a bit like a Michelin tyre; her bun rested on her hair, her cheeks rested on her chins, her chins rested on her chest, her chest rested on her stomach and all in all she was like one great spinning top in ever-increasing circles. And equally merry and bright! In no time at all Effie had been shovelled into the kitchen, plunked down on a chair and given a cup of hot tea with an enormous soda scone liberally plastered with salty butter.

Mrs McConnachie then proceeded to draw up opposite her on an outsized pine wood rocking chair. Very carefully she arranged her skirts and lowered herself on to the seat. Immediately it tossed forward as though giving a large and dramatic bow; she might even have collapsed all together face down on the floor, had not her little feet quickly prevented the chair from swinging forward any further. Then, placing her large plump hands on her apron she proceeded to instruct Effie on what her duties would be: 'It won't be easy, my girl,' she said, 'he's a right tadger, the master. Don't I find that myself! Indeed, I'm exhausted every day just with the two or three things he keeps demanding to be done. You see, he's a bit, how do they say, en-sin-ter-ic.'

'Oh,' said Effie, 'eccentric,' as gently as she could.

'Aye, isn't that what I'm saying! He's got all these jam-jars full of specimens, things like that; there's bones cluttered here, there and everywhere – you never saw the like, and the dusting round about – he won't let you put a duster near the things that he's got on his desk! And all the time he's prowling around with his books. He's got books, books and books, and I'm sure the half of the contents is evil. I think he's indulging in the black magic or something like that. I don't know, he's supposed to be a scientist, but if that's science I'd rather not have anything to do with it myself! But there it is. I just do his cooking and his cleaning as best I can. I think it'll be your job to look after some of those specimens for him. At any rate, I'll send you in and see what he thinks, if he thinks you can manage to sort them out. I'll just do that!'

And in the late afternoon she knocked gently on the huge, wooden door. A gruff voice said, 'What do you want?'

Mrs McConnachie said, 'The new girl has arrived. Did you want to see her?'

The voice answered, 'Send her in, woman!' And the next thing Effie knew was the door being opened and Mrs McConnachie roughly shoving her inside.

At first, the room was so dark she could hardly see anything. There was a huge window. But it was curtained from the outside by naked trees, trees that looked like Brillo pads, not a leaf on them; dark, sinister and touching from time to time the panes of grubby glass that had never been cleaned in years, hung on the inside with cobwebs where large spiders were busy at work. Some of them suddenly darting down towards the sill, then clambering up again and weaving their magnificent traps for flies. Some of these spiders' webs contained already a number of flies. A horrifying sight, Effie thought. There were huge, dark, green, velvet curtains hung either side of this window, looped up with great, big, thick, rope-like objects with tassels on the end. Effie had never seen these before – Victorian curtain loops they were, in fact. Then she drew her eyes from the scanty light of the window to the occupier of the room. He stood behind an enormous table so cluttered the objects on it reached up to his chin.

A tall man, with greyish-red hair, he looked lopsided in some strange way. His neck was to the one side; very red, very long, with a loose collar at its base. Above that was a stubbly chin with ginger whiskers all over it, and a loose, red, wet, hanging mouth. The nose was protruding and so were the enormous ears, jutting out either side like propellers on a ship. He was no maiden's dream, that's for sure! He also wore spectacles, also hanging to the one side. The whole effect was of someone leaning to starboard. Effie was now drawn to his hands. They were quite enormous, busily dissecting a rabbit laid out on a grubby newspaper. In the one hand he held what looked like a scout knife, a small carving knife, and with the other he held the poor animal's legs in a vicious grip while he gutted it with obvious relish, his mouth still grinning, the corners turned upwards.

He took no notice whatsoever of Effie at first, he was so absorbed in this hideous task, so she was able to cast her glance around the rest of the room. The fireplace arrested her; there was no lit fire, but a great string hung across the mantle shelf. From it hung all sorts of creatures: weasels, stoats, blackbirds, herons, rats – even rats! It was a horrific sight. She very nearly put up on the spot. She controlled herself quickly and threw her gaze towards a high chiffonier effect, a mahogany cupboard, really, with shelves in it. On every shelf were rows and rows of jars; and inside, objects that looked like tadpoles, but could have been anything. Some of them looked like naked eyes, very weird, a terrible collection: some were highly coloured, green and red. The whole room smelt heavily almost making her sick, reminding her of mothballs and nail varnish remover, or, perhaps it was pear drops – a strange, acrid stink. In a way, she couldn't help being re-minded of her grandmother's fur, which had been stowed under the bed in a tin trunk for years and years – the same sort of musty, horrible smell that would give anyone nightmares.

The only thing that seemed in any way normal was one of the walls, lined with bookshelves, right up to the ceiling; all kinds of books – tall leather-bound ones, paperbacks, all in disarray, none in order, tall ones, long ones, short ones, all piled in higgledy piggledy. And it turned out that this was the first job that Professor Arkley gave her. For that was his name: he was a Sassenach all right. He asked her to come the following morning at eight o'clock and put all his books in order.

He indicated which ones he wanted on one shelf, and which he wanted on another. She had to dust them thoroughly, clean them up, put them in the correct order. This she was quite pleased to do. Having given these instructions, he showed no further interest in the girl whatsoever. She waited and waited. He never looked at her, talked to her or anything.

So, after a while she said, 'Is that all, sir?'

And he said, 'Oh, are you still there? Off you go – clear out!' She flew for her life, never so glad to get out of a room in her life.

She grovelled her way to the kitchen and Mrs McConna-chie promptly put another cup of tea into her still trembling hand. 'Dear me, dear me,' said the old girl, 'you look as if you'd seen a ghost.'

'He's pretty fearsome right enough,' said Effie, swallowing her tea.

'Ach well, you'll maybe get used to his ways through time.'

As time went on Effie was perfectly certain she would never ever get used to his ways, to this horrible old manse or to the tasks he gave her. For one thing, he expected her to have read or understood the books that he'd put her in charge of. She'd never read anything other than the Bible in her life before, except for the few schoolbooks she had taken home for homework. She wasn't what you would call well read, and eventually it dawned on him that she was illiterate. He insisted on her taking a book with her every time she left the room, studying it in the evening and bringing it back to him the following day with her comments.

In this way, it's true, Effie did learn a lot about subjects in which she had no real interest – at first. But then gradually things began to take hold of her, especially books on the occult, books on archaeology, geology and some of the descriptions given; the illustrations in the books were very close to home. Books about Skara Brae, Carloway and all the standing stones that she had heard about previously intrigued her, very much so. It was fascinating to read about the druids, the burnt sacrifices; intriguing to learn about people being buried alive, rising up again in the middle of the night and the full moon shining down on their white faces. There were also books with recipes: how to cure chilblains, toothache; how to make a potion that would make you look more attractive; potions that would make you fall in love or be loved, change the colour of your hair; endless things one could learn. And gradually she did so.

Not that there was all that much time for cleaning anyway, as the old manse was large and difficult to clean. The bathroom, for instance: the bath was made of solid copper and it was her duty to polish that every single day. She also had to clean out the kitchen sinks, sweep and hose round about the back door where the wild goats would come and make a mess all over the doorstep. And that damned cat, well! She had no words to express her disgust for that animal. Then there were hens leaving their droppings here, there and everywhere, and often getting right inside the kitchen. She had to chase them through the pantries and the old stone larders, and would find them laying their eggs in all sorts of strange places, once in the meal barrel.

She was thankful about one thing, though, and that was her boss, the professor, seemed to ignore her completely. He never noticed when she came in the room and he never noticed when she went out. It was as though she didn't exist; she was glad of that because she could not in any way like such a man. But she did like Maggie McConnachie and got very fond of the old woman. So it came as a great shock one day towards spring when Donald the Post came to the door; came in, sat down, had his scone and tea, and produced of all things a telegram – for Maggie McConnachie. She nearly fainted, had to be held up before she would risk opening it; a telegram always meant a death or bad news of some sort. And indeed it was bad news; Maggie's sister had taken ill suddenly, had been put into hospital in Stornoway. And her family had asked that Maggie go to her immediately, as there was not much possibility of her recovering. Now this was a dilemma that no one had anticipated.

Effie was shattered. But Maggie McConnachie was quite confident, even eager to go, as soon as possible. 'You'll manage fine,' she said to Effie. 'I taught you to cook, you can even cook scones, my dear. You'll manage excellently, I'm quite sure of it; you're the cleanest wee soul we've had about the house ever. I'm sure he'll be very pleased with all the results. And I'll get back as soon as I possibly can.' It was a great relief, however, when Donald the Post said he would get his wife to come up and give Effie a hand for a day or two at least.

But Donald's wife never showed up, neither did Donald, so poor Effie was left alone in this ghastly old house with this ghastly old man. Never exchanging a word with him day after day and night after night. She would creep up the wooden stairs with her book under her arm to her isolated little room with a skylight, up in the attic, all the boards in the landing creaking as she made her way to her miserable little room. It had been a storeroom and there still remained within it glass cages and glass domes with stuffed birds in them. The bed itself was mounted high with wrought iron bed-ends that resembled church gates, like something you might see outside the Vatican they were so elaborate. And they cast a sinister shadow on the whitewashed walls that were already yellow with stains and damp. Effie's mind formed images – images of people, animals frightening her – reducing her to floods of tears. She would collapse on the floor, pull out her little green suitcase and start to pack. She hadn't a clue in the world how she would go about running away. But it was her firm intention to do so.

The night before she left, however, something absolutely dreadful happened, so appalling it would have been better had it been a nightmare. It was a night when the half-moon threw its light through the skylight onto a patch in the middle of the ugly lino. She sat there with her book and had lit a candle, so that she could see the better. There was no electricity in the house at all; only oil lamps and candles. So, tears running down her face, feeling very exhausted as she'd worked very hard all day, she crouched down on the cold ugly lino, trying to read a book she would have to describe the following day when she went into his office to clean and dust.

The time of the half-moon would worry Effie a lot: some-times she thought it looked like a face, a protruding nose and a sharp chin. It reminded her of that horrible old man down-stairs, of whom she felt an instinctive fear and dread. Espe-cially being alone as she was. So it wasn't surprising to her at any rate when she heard the old wooden staircase begin to creak. She knew every step of it. She knew that he'd got to the bend in the stairs, she knew that he hesitated there. Then the footsteps became louder and she knew he'd reached the second landing. She made her way quickly to the door, but there was no key and no way of locking it. She thought about putting a chair against it, but by the time she'd grabbed a chair he had already reached the door. She put her foot and her body against it, but he soon pushed her aside, roughly, making her collapse onto the linoleum-covered floor.

'What do you want?' she said. 'Get out – I-I don't like anybody coming in my room!'

He laughed, with an ugly laugh, and said, 'Oh well, whether you like it or not, my girl, I've just come up to have a chat with you and see, eh, what, ah, you're reading. I was curious to know which book you'd taken this evening.'

'Here you are, here you are!' she said, shoving the book at him. 'You can take it, take it away! Please, go!'

'Oh,' he said, 'no fear, I'm not going now. I've taken the trouble to climb up these stairs, so I'll stay up these stairs.' And with that he grabbed her, shoved her on the bed. She was absolutely terrified. He yanked off his tie and bound her wrists together, tied them to the wrought iron bed-ends. Slowly, she began to lose consciousness. Her imagination took over; she thought that the great big golden eagle in the corner of the room had smashed its glass and flown up towards the ceiling, hovered there, then come swooping down upon her, its outspread wings covering her and its beak protruding, jabbing into her body. There was no use scream-ing, no use, nothing she could do. There was no way in which she could be saved from this hideous monster.

When he left her she tumbled to the floor and crawled on hands and knees towards the rickety iron stand that held the old-fashioned ewer and basin. The ewer contained some freezing water. With this water she bathed, mopping up the blood, dabbing the bruises, trying to soothe her eye, her mouth, her body, weeping aloud and hearing her own heart thudding, thudding loudly, loud, rapidly thudding in her body. Her sobbing was exhausting her but she would not sleep, would not stay another moment in this dreadful place. She completed the packing of her suitcase, not forgetting the childish little rag book that she loved better than any other. It would never mean the same to her now. For she herself was no longer a child. Roughly, crudely, viciously, she'd been flung into an adult world.

It was beginning to be light when she grovelled her way down the wooden staircase once more. She tiptoed towards the big front door, opened it silently. Then down the steps, along the path and hurriedly on and on till she came to the little bridge. The river was in full spate, the sun beginning to rise over the distant mountains. She would have four miles at least to walk, lumbering the suitcase, before she reached the outskirts of the village, and found her way, stumbling blindly, to the pier, to wait for the early steamer which came from the Outer Isles. She didn't know where she would go, what she would do; she had her money, her wages and the little that she had drawn from the post office before taking the job. So there was enough to pay her fare and get her on a train that would take her somewhere, anywhere, away from this terrible place and these terrible memories which a lifetime would never clear from her mind.

Effie Mathieson was a God-fearing Christian. She'd been brought up that way, but it didn't stop her from being very superstitious; she believed in all sorts of signs and had read much of the occult, the mysteries of life. There was the half-moon, which always meant something for her; a change, a difference. There was the figure eight that played a great part in her life. There were signs and signals which she drew on to guide her, advise her on what and what not to do. So, after leaving the steamer at Kyle of Lochalsh and boarding a train she eventually found herself in Inverness.

Effie Mathieson from Glen Conon in Skye had arrived all by herself in Inverness, without a clue where she could stay or how she could contact her aunt, her mother's sister, whom she knew lived here. Effie knew her and her cousin Kirsty well, because they used to come to Skye, stay in the summer, when Effie's own mother and father were alive and living on their croft in Glen Conon. So how was she going to go about finding them? She vaguely remembered the address, eight something, and then she realised she would have to find a hotel as it was getting late. Fortunately, she had often heard her father talk about the drovers coming down from Skye to the market in Inverness with their sheep and their cattle; she'd heard him often talk about the hospitality the men received when they stayed in The Drovers' Inn. The proprietor Mr Douglas had been a keen farmer in his day and was very good to all the men who came down from the island. He gave them a cut price to stay in their hotel, making his profits mainly in the bar. So, Effie enquired of someone who looked like a policeman where this inn was, and he directed her there.

The proprietor almost hugged her: he too had visited Skye and had seen Effie as an infant many years ago. Mr Douglas was full of compliments as to how she had blossomed into such a lovely young lady. Effie was not used to praise and blushed to the roots of her hair. Regretfully, Douglas said they were full up, but he could give her, if she didn't mind, a room in the servants' quarters above the bar. This she eagerly accepted. He helped her in with her little green suitcase. She had many stairs to climb before reaching what seemed like an attic.

He said, 'You'll be all right, quite safe, because the girls all sleep up here at night. There'll be two girls in the room next to you so you don't have to worry, you can always bang on the wall! There will be a lot of noise because men are loud when they're drinking, unfortunately.'

Effie lost no time in settling into her room. But she hadn't counted on the noise made below: clanking of glasses, banging of fists, raucous laughter going on nearly all night. Her limbs were limp and tired, she had an awful lot to think about, so she just lay there, once or twice worrying when she heard the girls coming up to their rooms. Footsteps on the staircase immediately threw her mind back to the terrifying footsteps in the manse at Glen Conon. But she cast it all aside, made plans for what she would do. In the morning, after a hearty breakfast, she asked Douglas if he knew where her aunt was now living.

He said, 'Oh dear me, poor girl, did you not hear? She died last March.' And this shook Effie considerably.

'And her daughter,' she said, 'where is Kirsty?'

'Oh, Kirsty's all right,' said Douglas. 'She's gone off to Glasgow to do nursing. She's in the Western Infirmary enjoying her career very much. You should be able to find her quite easily if you're intending to proceed to Glasgow.'

'Oh, I am,' said Effie, 'I am!' And Douglas kindly took her to the station the following morning to catch the early train.

She found an empty carriage and was able to catch up on some of the sleep she'd lost during the night when she'd had to listen to all the stories the men were cracking with each other. Old stories she'd heard before . . . one about the old drunken drover from Kylerhea who was taking so long groping in his pockets for enough money to pay for his whisky, having spent nearly all he possessed at the sales and getting so little in return for his money. In those days, they would only get about two shillings a head for the sheep. And it was heart-breaking, they would go home, vow that they would never try to bring sheep to the market, any more.

The drover was fumbling around for his money in his pocket. The barman was getting irate and impatient: 'Hurry up,' he said, 'hurry up, I haven't got all day!'

And old Dougie said, 'Ah well, wait now, wait, man! I can't find my money that easy – I've got so many troubles – and my heid is just full of "beasts". And me telling this tale.' The men at the bar would laugh their heads off, politely, to encourage the old boy.

The monotonous movement of the fast-moving express train would make her sleep fitfully, then wake in terror: what was she doing, where was she going, how could she survive not knowing anybody? Well, she did know Kirsty, or, could vaguely remember her. The last time she'd seen Kirsty they were just little girls playing on the croft, enjoying themselves. She had a vivid picture in her mind of herself and her cousin sitting on the long grass picking daisies, making long daisy chains, winding them round each other's necks. Those peaceful, lovely days with her mother, her father and friends; how suddenly and rapidly it had all changed, leaving her as an orphan to fend for herself. There was some money that she would inherit when she was twenty-one, but that was a good way off yet, money due to her for the sale of their land and croft house. She had no brothers or sisters so she would not be without funds.

Effie was so glad of the carriage to herself, and indulged in reminiscences, trying to pick out the pleasant ones in order to squeeze out the horror that still lingered in her mind. She would remember the time when she and Kirsty used to take their shoes and socks off, paddle in the ditches at the side of the road round about the drinking well looking for frogs; one day Effie took one home. When her mother saw it she had said, 'Oh you stupid girl. Take that straight back! Don't you know if you bring a frog back to the house with you, it'll get into your ear in the night and sleep there.' Hearing this Effie had run back to the ditch with the poor, wee frog. She would smile to herself; it was comforting to think of these episodes in her young days, before the tragedy of losing her mother and father . . .

After four or more hours the train pulled into Central Station, Glasgow. This was a fantastic experience for Effie. She thought the station magnificent, like some great cathedral she'd read about; the amazing ornate roof that covered the entire space; the shouting and calling of porters; the bustle of human beings, so many people rushing for trains or disembarking from them. At the same time she felt utterly lost, not knowing which way to turn. And in the end she thought her best plan would be to find a tea-shop, have something to eat and drink, then find another policeman, and ask him where the Western Infirmary was, so she could seek out her cousin.

Effie was in luck; she saw a taxi and was driven within ten minutes to this big hospital. She found her way to the main gate and trotting up to it asked a white-coated doctor, or student, she did not know, how she could find her cousin who was a nurse in this same hospital. He very kindly propelled her along the corridors till they came to a door that had the name of the matron printed on it. He knocked and, turning the handle, shoved her gently in.

The matron said sharply, 'What do you want? What are you doing here?' Effie stuttered out that she had come down from the Isle of Skye and was seeking her cousin, a nurse in this hospital.

'The Isle of Skye?' said the matron. 'Oh well, isn't that

where I come from myself! When did you arrive?"

Effie said she'd just arrived, had got a taxi up to the hospital and didn't know Glasgow at all. The matron made her sit down, asked her a lot about herself and lost no time in fetching Kirsty.

The two girls embraced each other and together left the matron when five o'clock came round. Emotion with both girls was magnetic. Poor Effie could hardly get her breath, had been for so long adrift in an open sea with nothing to hang on to since her mother and father had passed on, and it was the same with Kirsty. Kirsty's mother had been ill for a long time with cancer, had had a lot of treatment travelling back and forward from Inverness to Glasgow, till finally she'd moved to Glasgow with her daughter to go more frequently and easily to the Western Infirmary. And that was how it came about that Kirsty, who stood by her mother night and day, took a notion to become a nurse herself. She applied and was accepted. And that is how she also had a flat in Glasgow, where she and her mother had lived up to her mother's death.

The flat was in a very large building near to the Broomie-law, hard up against the Clyde and not very far from the Hielandman's Umbrella, on the corner of Argyle Street. It was called this because here lonely Highlanders would meet, talk Gaelic and commiserate with each other, be homesick and make plans for catching the train home. Effie was no longer depressed! She now had her beloved cousin, and the two girls clung to each other thirstily. Effie was with part of her own flesh and blood, Kirsty hugging and kissing and welcoming her. The two girls needed each other; a pair of orphans with the same background, both spoke Gaelic and they prattled in the language till they were exhausted.

It soon transpired that Kirsty, after several weeks on night duty, was allowed a forty-eight hour pass of freedom. She planned to take Effie to the flat and install her. There were five rooms, large and spacious. One of them was let to a Spanish lady, an elderly woman. This old dear was a wardrobe mistress: a beautiful seamstress who could make garments and alter them in no time at all. And so she was engaged by most of the theatres to do the costumes, alter, attend, iron and have them ready when needed for the various plays put on in the splendid theatres all round Glasgow. There were not many shows on at the moment, so the rest of the flat was empty. Normally, Kirsty would rent out to actresses and actors, travelling folk, the remainder of the rooms.

Effie was intrigued with these houses up a close. Where she came from the houses were usually built by the families themselves, detached, built of solid stone with peat smoke coming from their chimneys, set in open crofts, some lonely and isolated. But here there were human beings living all in the one building in different flats – a ground floor flat, then a first, a second, then a third floor flat, and sometimes a fourth – all joined together by a magnificent banister, shiny and polished, that ran all the way up through the middle of the building. Little brass knobs were set here and there all the way down the banister. She presumed that that was to prevent anyone from sliding down as the children often tried to do.

When they reached Kirsty's flat, she opened the big, solid front door with a letter-box and big lion's head knocker. They entered and were greeted by the little seamstress, Maria Martinas. She ushered them into her compartment, insisted on their sitting down and having a warm cup of coffee.

When Effie had said she liked the idea of the closes Maria said, 'Oh dear me, they can be a bit spooky! Especially at night with only a gas light down there, and courting couples coming in, thinking they were alone and would be undisturbed. But the children got wise to them in number one, the flat above here. They would collect tin cans, tying string round them, dangling them over the wooden banister from the top of the house, jangling and bashing them against the railings to frighten the lovers below inside the close – causing them to pull themselves together, tidy up their attire and fly for their lives, shamefaced and so astonished, thinking they were being pursued by a bunch of banshees!'

When Kirsty and Effie accepted Maria Martinas's invitation to have coffee Effie was astonished at the cosiness and the difference of this lady's room. She'd read about Spain and France in books back in Glen Conon, but she didn't expect to experience this very different atmosphere. The room was charming with soft-coloured walls and velvet curtains; a very Spanish-looking place with dark oak furniture, very ornate; great carved dressers with a candelabra sitting on its centre and a bowl of violets at its side. There was of course an icon above the door, for Maria was an ardent Catholic, and to crown it all a most magnificent painting in the centre of the whole wall. She'd seen in picture books paintings by Velazquez and she presumed that this was a copy of one. The biscuits and cake were delicious; Maria had made them herself. The conversation was stimulating. Kirsty was in good form, glad to have a little respite from her night duty. She said some of it had been very hard going.

One night she'd had what they call 'night nurse's paralysis'. She told how she was sitting by a small table in a ward with six men, and in the middle of the night one of them demanded a urine bottle. Kirsty, who was very quick to attend to any patient needing anything, was so conscientious she tried to leap up from her chair and her knitting to help the man – but found she couldn't move. This was a terrifying experience – a man crying out to her and she couldn't raise herself from the chair. It seemed as if this went on for an eternity, when fortunately a nursing sister happened to be passing and looked in. So, thank goodness, Kirsty was relieved. She also told of a time during the war when she had to attend to a seriously injured patient, his burns so bad they were all over his body. She was exhausted beyond belief, but got on her knees and started to bathe, treat and bandage his feet. She worked at that, didn't know where her strength was coming from, bandaged all up one leg and then the other and on to the torso. On and on she bandaged and bathed. When at last she looked up, she said to her astonishment, 'My God, the bugger is dead!' Maria was a bit shocked with that one, but secretly Effie couldn't help thinking it was rather funny.

Maria chatted away merrily too, telling of her upbringing in Spain which was very, very strict; her parents were horrified when tourism started. Many Spaniards were very impoverished and glad of tourism but were mortified to see women and men parading about in next to nothing; bikinis were all the rage and true Spaniards were very shocked. So much so that Maria's parents decided to send her away from Spain to Paris to a finishing school, where she learned to pour tea from a silver teapot and other refinements, and was expected to come home a very polished and refined young lady. Instead of that, she climbed through a window one night and went to a dance with a boy from a neighbouring school. Well, she wasn't exactly expelled, but she did leave and went to art school instead, where she studied dress design and finally ended up as a wardrobe mistress to the Comédie Française. Since then she'd been freelance, and was currently sorting and packing costumes for a travelling circus.

Time was running on, the night closing in, but Effie, looking through the window in the half-light, was intrigued by a lovely old tree growing on the edge of the pavement all by itself. Its branches had been clipped, causing the tree to be shaped rather like the head of a señorita, draped with a lace mantilla. The evening light shining through the lace was giving it a magic Effie found very pleasing. They then went up to an apartment that would be Effie's home for some of the future.

It was large and very theatrical, one wall covered entirely with photographs of stars and starlets dating back from Gladys Cooper and Greta Garbo right up to the present day; masses of them all pinned up on the wall. Her attention was then drawn to the window. When she pushed the curtain aside her excitement was beyond belief, like opening up a Christmas stocking. Her rooms were on the top floor and there was a sea of different-shaped, different-coloured roofs, some mounted by dozens and dozens of chimney pots all shapes and sizes – tall, short, thin, fat, some badly stained, some broken and cracked, leaning sideways, all had personalities! They seemed to reach from where she was right down to the Broomielaw and the Clyde. This was sheer magic. All her life she'd looked upon the machair and the sea and the mountains. She'd never seen a scene like this before, and she had an urge to paint it. Then she couldn't paint. But that was soon rectified.

Through time she converted her attic home into a studio. And Maria Martinas, having gone to art school in Paris, very kindly volunteered to teach Effie all the ins and outs of being an artist. Eventually Effie was accepted backstage with the various theatrical companies that came to Glasgow. She worked with Maria painting scenery and arranging sets, working as an assistant stage manager, even went on tour and enjoyed the life immensely. She took on small parts understudying, and was thrilled when one day she was asked to find a painting of an extremely ugly man – they were going to take Oscar Wilde's play *Portrait of Dorian Gray* to Paris.

They couldn't find an ugly enough painting to take with them. So, Effie volunteered to paint one herself. She knew better than anyone else in the world exactly which face was the ugliest, without doubt.

So, she proceeded to paint Professor Arkley, the fiend who had attacked her. And she painted feverishly; it took only three days, she couldn't stop once she'd started. And in the end she had the spitting image of that hideous man.

So, they all went to Paris. And for Effie this was a wonderful experience, sniffing the air in the Champs Elysées. She thought to herself, 'This is just like champagne. It's wonderful, I love this place!' And she got to know many of the artists who displayed their work on the Left Bank. She enjoyed the people, the friendship and the camaraderie amongst the artistic groups, felt that this was a place she would like to spend the rest of her life in. But then she had from Kirsty a joyful letter: she'd been going for some time with a doctor in the hospital and he had proposed to her. She now had decided that she would like to marry and settle down. Could Effie come back for the wedding in September? Well, of course, Effie was only too eager to go to her cousin's wedding!

Maria would make her a beautiful bridesmaid's dress. And it so happened that on the last night of the show of Dorian Gray in Paris there was an art dealer in the audience. He came backstage and offered a substantial sum of money for the portrait of Dorian Gray. So, the theatre asked Effie if she was prepared to part with it. She said she was only too glad! The dealer showed it first in the Paris salon, then removed it and took it with him to America, to Wisconsin. This was a great relief for Effie, because there is an old Highland saying that 'if something had a buidseach on it, a curse or a spell, if you took it across the oceans over the sea, the spell would be dispelled'.

She went back happily to her flat in Glasgow where she

could enjoy painting in her studio, listening to the children in the communal yard below. Occasionally she would see some damn fool woman placing her enormous posterior on the outside of a window ledge and proceeding to clean the window with a chamois leather, risking her life and little girls jumping on to the top of the Anderson Shelter that had been built in the War and skipping and singing their rhymes:

> Oh dear me
> My granny caught a flea
> She peppered it and salted it
> And took it to her tea.

And the old drunk who came by occasionally clinging on to the roan pipes and singing his guts out, 'O for the Wings of a Dove'. Effie thought he must have in his youth been a cat burglar. The kind Glaswegians would chuck buttons and ha'pennies down on his head, and he would stagger off to sing in another close.

But, like most Highlanders, Effie Mathieson would endeavour to spend her last days back in An t-Eilean Sgitheanach:

> Jerusalem, Athens and Rome
> I would see them before I would die
> But I'd rather not see any one of the three
> Than be exiled forever from Skye.

Northern Lights

The Swivel

When Annie MacKinnon went to milk the cows in the barn one lovely sunny morning she was astounded to find a bundle wrapped in ship's canvas lying amongst the clean hay of an unused stall. The bundle was neatly wrapped, made fast with a length of rope tied securely to an udalain – and for those of you who don't speak Gaelic, an udalain is an iron ring held by another iron ring and wedged into the stone wall with a big square iron nail. This makes it mobile, and on to this swivel a rope is attached to tether the cows. Poor Annie was so taken by surprise all she could do was wring her hands and chant over and over again, 'Obh, obh obh*,' the poor wee thing tied to an udalain!' – and in that way the name stuck. The little baby boy she'd found tethered there came to be known as Angus the Udalain.

Now, because of the kind of gear he had been trussed up in, his Aunt Annie came to the conclusion his father must have gone to sea, and somehow or other forgotten to come back. So, who he was remained a mystery. Annie however did her duty by the boy, gave him a good Christian upbringing, and filled his head with stories from the New Testament which he seemed to enjoy the best. His great ambition was to become a fisherman, as he thought his father must have been. And, being a little, shall we say, uninhibited, he would often wander down to the shore and start shouting instructions to fishing

* Obh, obh obh – Oh, what a shame!

boats: 'Keep her prow in the wind there, man!' or 'Cast your nets to the starboard side!' Once he tried shutting his eyes tight, forcing himself to believe that he wouldn't drown if he walked right off the end of the jetty on to the water. Fortunately for him, there was another lad there to throw him a rope!

He had a good singing voice, too, and liked to imagine that the wind and the sea would carry his song far out, maybe to the other end of the world. Now don't run away with the idea that he was lazy or trying to avoid work, for he was very helpful always, would give anyone a hand to bring in the hay or do a bit of digging. But his heart was always at sea.

Well, one day working away in the turnip field he felt unhappy and disgruntled – turnips, how he hated them. There was no money in them either, not worth cultivating except to make lantern heads for Hallowe'en. The soup his auntie made with them stuck in his gullet. Stretching himself and raising his face to catch a passing shower against his brow, he marvelled at the vivid beauty of a rainbow above his head, the unbroken curve of blue and red and green dipping down over the mountains and into the river. What a power was there – if God could do that He could do anything. Was it true, he wondered, what they said –'at the end of a rainbow lay a pot o' gold'? He wished it were, but then why shouldn't it be? Had anyone ever investigated? If his auntie expected him to believe in miracles, the Books of Isaiah and Revelations, then why should he not believe in this?

Dropping his turnip, his eyes glued, fascinated, to the end of the rainbow, the Udalain walked up as though in a dream to the road that led to the River Rha. It was a good way, mind you, and his wellington boots were cumbersome; but some driving force was egging him on towards the rainbow's end – when he got there, there was no end. The river was in full spate, a seagull was resting contentedly on a boulder stuck up high and dry above the water that was fiercely embracing it. Well, no one could dig here; there might be a trout or two, but it hardly amounted to a crock of gold. He would try further on where the colours seemed to be evaporating into the mountainside. On and on he trudged, inspired by what we might call a hunch, but all he met were two young roe deer that had recently changed colour. The last time he had seen them they were a warm, cinnamon brown. Now they were dark, with stark white backsides anticipating no doubt a snowy winter. 'There could be money in them,' he thought, had he had a gun, which he hadn't; and even if he had, they were far too young to shoot.

Weary and depressed he knocked the lichen whiskers off an old tree stump and sat down. In doing so he had turned himself facing homewards, and it was then that he saw for the first time that the other end of the rainbow was dancing merrily over his auntie's rooftop. 'Chi nam beannaichean!'* he exclaimed in Gaelic, 'what a glaoich I am who doesn't know that a rainbow must have two ends, and I should have investigated the nearest one first!' So he made his way home at the double – there must be something waiting at home for him. He knew there must be something! And when he did reach home his aunt was waiting for him at the gate in a state of great agitation.

'For heaven's sake, Udalain, where have you been? Look at you! Go into the kitchen right away and tidy yourself! Take off those filthy boots! There's a man here from Inverness, he's waiting to see you down in the room' – and pausing for a moment she heaved her bosoms in an effort to get more breath – 'it's . . . it's about your father, you see, it appears you've got one after all.'

* Chi nam beannaichean! – Over the top (I see the light)!

'My father!' shouted the Udalain, for he couldn't believe his ears.

'Yes, yes, you'll hear all about it from the gentleman himself,' she said and shoved him down to the bare little room that was only used at communion time.

Well, it appears that his father had come from the mainland, having emigrated to California nineteen years ago, leaving his wife and six children to follow him out after he had found a job. This had taken a lot longer than it should have done. The poor wife was nearly demented and began to think he wasn't going to send for them at all. She was in a terrible state with no food or clothing for all those children, except for what the neighbours handed out to her.

So think of her dilemma when she realised she was going to have a seventh child! When she wrote and told her husband he wrote back and said he'd only bargained for six kids; if she thought of bringing another one out then she needn't come at all. And that's how she came to take the poor wee Udalain some distance away so that no one would suspect her. She had been to school with Annie and knew well of her reputation for kindness. She had used the canvas to wrap the child in, as she had no other warm clothes to cover him with.

Now the tragic thing was that what she had done weighed heavily on her, she got ill in mind and body because she had lied, telling her husband that the baby had died. It was not till she herself was lying on her deathbed that she confessed the truth – and this was him after all these years trying to make amends! You see, his other children had all left home when the mother died – some to Canada and some to New Zealand. They had all prospered very well and so indeed had he, for he now owned a large fruit farm, and this was him at last communicating with his son, sending him a large sum of money, enough to come out to California and live with himself, or to invest it in whatever way he chose. This then was the Udalain's 'crock of gold'. What he did with it I'll never know, for I never did hear the end of the story, more's the pity.

Welcome Home

Now that the days are drawing in, the fires being built up and the tongues wagging Skye is settling down to winter, taking it easy so to speak after a hard season of tourism and bed-and-breakfast. So now the natives can get together again to do their own thing, starting with the national Mod, local drama, going for a song and cailleachs telling stories true and false. 'Did you hear this?' and 'wait till I tell you that' will be on everyone's lips. Well, here goes . . .

Did you hear about Iain Mór and the pair of boots he found when he was chasing his cow out of Andy's croft one evening (the silly blighter, Andy had left the top gate open when he came to borrow methylated spirits for his toddy)? Iain's eye fell on a pair of quite good-looking boots tucked under the bracken. The trouble was, when he went to pick them up, weren't they still attached to the legs of an old man! Yes, stiff and cold and dead as mutton he was. Poor Iain got an awful shock, but he managed to get the doctor and helped to get the corpse shifted to the hospital all the same.

Yes, seemingly this was a man not unknown on the island: he'd got the call-up to the army when he was about twenty, had been drafted abroad. No one knew what had become of this Alexander MacSween until this summer when the poor old creatuir in old-fashioned clothes had chapped on every door on his native isle trying to get accommodation. The hotels wouldn't have him either, they were all booked up. 'Is it a single?' they'd say, looking at him down their nose (no posh car, no smart luggage, you see). 'Sorry, you should have booked earlier.'

How his heart must have ached and his feet, for no one would listen to him long enough to hear his story or find out who he was. Except for one woman who gave him a jug of warm milk and said he could spend the night in her barn. The situation was 'quite ludicrous', he thought to himself as he sat on a heap of hay and managed to chuckle in spite of the tears swelling on his eyelids ready to drop. These were his people, this greedy mercenary lot, this was his island, his home that he had dreamt of, cherished and loved for all these long years.

He watched the brown voles trotting in under the barn door. Like himself they needed shelter. One of them got too close and he thrust out his foot to chase it away. In doing so he struck too hard; he'd killed it, thoughtlessly, quite unintentionally. It too had only wanted warmth and shelter. At crack of dawn Alexander MacSween (son of Skye) continued on his way.

'Hey, Gillian, dear, did you see that wee man that went out just now? A proper crack-pot. He sent for me, the cheek, and said that if he couldn't get a room tonight he would like to buy the hotel. I told him to pull the other leg, then sent him off to see Menzies the solicitor, just for a laugh you know.'

But it was no laughing matter. Alexander MacSween, Boston, USA, industrial tycoon, shipping magnate (or maybe gangster extraordinaire) had come home, with his old clothes and his old memories that have no place in today's world. He did see the solicitor, it's true. Not to buy himself a roof, but to make out his will leaving twenty thousand pounds to a hostel in Manhattan. And, here's the rub, 'Five hundred pounds to Katie Andersen, number nine, South Cuil, Uig, Isle of Skye – who had been good enough to give him a jug of warm milk.'

The Lonely Loch

The loch was high up in the mountains. It was a strange place to build a hut, no doubt, but then Lachlan himself was a trifle strange. That's what happens when you are so mad about the fishing that you exclude all else from your life. Trout fishing, that was his favourite, and his downfall. Before he built the hut he used to ride up to the loch on a horse, but at this time of the year his father needed the horse for the ploughing; so, taking a supply of tinned foods, Lachlan decided to settle for a few months of uninterrupted fishing. Unfortunately, he had overlooked the fact that you cannot over-fish the most prolific loch.

He would stand for hours in rain and midges, the hunger gnawing at his guts and wishing he had a wife to care for his food and wash his linen. For the past seven hours he hadn't had a single bite from food or fish! He watched the ripples widening on the surface of the water, newly roused by the wake of a wild goose propelling its miniature young to the shelter of the long reeds; then lifted his eyes to a small island, hairy with bushes and trees that seemed always to be floating in the middle of the loch. (He had christened it the Sporran Isle, for that's what it reminded him of.) On the one side of it there grew a silver birch, its branches flung out like the spokes of a green parasol. And now he thought he saw someone on the island – but that was not possible, how could anyone get there?

The raft was still made fast beside him and no one had come up the mountain track for the past three weeks. He must be seeing things surely. No, he was right, it was a woman half hidden in the reeds like Nefertiti. Or was it a man, Narcissus perhaps? Was she bathing? Good gracious . . . well, Lachlan was a shy man and rather than embarrass himself or the stranger, he went back to his hut to open one of the few remaining tins he had left. From time to time he would peek out of the window to see if she or it was still there, or if he had dreamt it all. And sure enough, he could still see a shadow amongst the reeds.

Lachlan couldn't sleep all that night for worrying – perhaps the poor soul had got cramp, was ill, couldn't swim back – so at crack of dawn he took the raft over to the Sporran Isle to investigate. Yes, she was still there all right, and what an apparition, singing away in the reeds with a voice like an angel – and the rest of her, well, my, there are no words to describe such beauty. Lachlan felt faint at the sight of her and there were spots before his eyes, or was it the sunlight in the silver birch flickering shadows across her exquisite form? 'No mortal being could look like you,' he breathed aloud.

'I'm not mortal,' she retorted, somewhat curtly. 'I am Màiri an Uisge* and I've been here for centuries, if you'd like to know.'

'Ach, I meant no offence,' said Lachlan shyly. 'But could you not become a human, for a short time anyway?'

'Why should I?' said Màiri. 'You have to give to get, you know, and you have been pretty greedy, taking all the trout, haven't you?'

'Ach, but I'll never throw another line in this loch, if you'll only say you'll marry me – honest, I won't!'

'I seem to have heard that one somewhere before,' said Màiri an Uisge coldly, but Lachlan was undaunted, and after

* Màiri an Uisge – Mary of the Loch

rowing out to the island every day for about a week, became desperate. 'There must be some way of making you mortal, Màiri, mo ghaoil,' he said.

'Well, there is one way,' said Màiri, 'but it's a difficult one, difficult for you I mean.'

'Just you name it,' said Lachlan.

'Very well then, since you are so keen; there is only one way I could keep alive and that's by swallowing one pearl every day, and you know yourself how few there are in this loch. It wouldn't be worth it.'

'It would, it would,' said Lachlan desperately, and started in to work straight away, opening up the oysters from the scanty beds and dragging home sacks full of mussels; for no matter how small the pearl, it would be one day more of love and life with Màiri.

Well, they were ideally happy for a time, as you can imagine, in spite of the shells and the guts mounting daily, lying mouldering in a heap at the side of the hut (idyllic love heeds no such thing). But, unfortunately, through time, she was wanting two pearls a day, saying that the climate wasn't agreeing with her. Poor Lachlan was desperate for food himself, as he had long since finished the last of the tins, and the distance to his home was so great he could only go there very infrequently and for as short a time as possible. He shrank from telling his folk at home of his life with Màiri, and he was terrified of leaving her alone for any length of time lest she should disappear again. He had diligently found for her a large supply of pearls, a small fortune in fact.

So, you can imagine his anger and distress when one day after a miserable trip home, and a hard trek back through the mountains, there was Màiri entertaining a gentleman, an English tourist at that, who had got permission to fish the loch! He had come up on horseback, well supplied with salmon sandwiches made from large thick pancakes filled with lettuce and mayonnaise, a flask of whisky and two bottles of wine. Màiri, who had never tasted wine before, was squiffy and fawning over the fellow like a long lost lover.

Lachlan was beside himself with rage and jealousy; he ordered the man to get out of his hut immediately, pelting him across the face with a large speckled trout, the nearest thing to hand. Well, Màiri's reaction was a truly feminine one. She gathered all the pearls into the fancy apron that Lachlan had stolen for her from his mother's wardrobe, then she ran after the man screaming and crying as if it were she that had been abused. Suddenly, the stranger halted, and turning, lifted her on to his horse, riding away into the falling dusk for all the world like young Lochinvar – leaving poor Lachlan alone, staring at the dust subsiding on the white hill track with nothing but the stench of rotten shells in his nostrils; the sure knowledge in his head, though, that once the pearls were gone, Màiri an Uisge would some day be back where she belonged.

Camisutory

Camisutory was a wee man without much stamina. That's why they gave him a big name. Mind you, he was a good wee soul and kindness itself. The funny thing was, all the rest of his family were great big whoppers, except for his father, who was small like himself. His two brothers were over six feet, and his sister, well, my goodness, her statistics were a good 42"-37"-42". They were all as dull as they were big, only Camisutory and his father had the brains. They were also very close friends. So, when the old man took pneumonia through wandering about at night – no one knew why or where – Camisutory was very upset and sat by his bedside continuously.

'My son,' said his father, 'I have something to tell you and don't let on to the others what it's about.'

Camisutory drew close to the old man, for he was wandering in his fever and rather incoherent, sitting up and chanting the 23rd Psalm one minute and panting for breath the next.

'Listen, my son,' he whispered mysteriously between verses, 'you and I are throwbacks . . . descended from wee folk that used to live underground . . . your brothers, they take after their mother . . . haven't got the gift. When I am gone, you go down to the end of the croft, you will see seven small hillocks close to the dyke where the weasels are. Go at night when there is no one about . . . try a wee dance . . . a badaibh-bàth on the top of the biggest hillock. Take your chanter with you, if you want, for they like music, and gradually you will feel the ground beneath your feet moving aside . . . like . . . like an eyelid opening . . .'

'My, but he is in a bad way,' thought Camisutory, 'poor man.'

'Wait . . . wait a minute, lad, I'm not finished yet . . . for it's there that you'll meet the Oracle, a wee fellow just like ourselves. He is really a ban-sìth, but don't tell him that, he would be offended . . . Now, any problem you might have, put it squarely to him. And when your time may come to die, impart the knowledge to your smallest son as I have done to you.' With that the old man tried another stanza and breathed his last.

Now, Camisutory didn't believe a word of all this. It was obvious his father had been havering under the strain of the fever. Till one day he saw a weasel chasing after one of the hens. As he ran to grab hold of the hen he stumbled over one of the hillocks, and remembered the yarn his father had told him. So that night, after dark, he took his chanter and strolled down there again, just for the hell of it. He could see the biggest hillock all right, arched black like an eyebrow against the white moonlight. Reaching the top of it he started to dance, gently at first, then wildly as he composed a rousing tune on his chanter.

'Hey, take it easy there, you'll have my roof off!' a small voice squawked. Camisutory felt the short sea grass moving from under his feet (a sensation like an escalator, only, of course, he had never seen an escalator in all his life). Camisutory was not all together surprised to find a wee man, not unlike himself, standing close beside him. He had a pleasant, welcoming expression on his face as he extended his hand, 'Camisutory, I believe? I have been expecting you. Come away in.'

And before Camisutory had time to say yea or nay, he found

himself sliding down a narrow passage, landing with a thump in a charming but dimly lit room. Instead of the oil lamps, candles or crùisgeans you would expect to find, there were jars glowing with a phosphorus substance fixed on the walls. The seats were slabs of stone and the beds were stone shelves scattered with sweet-smelling hay. In the centre of the room was a stone table set for what looked like a meal; the plates were large leaves and shells, though what was on them Camisutory couldn't rightly make out.

'Is it true they call you the Oracle?' began Camisutory nervously.

'That's right, I can give you advice on most things, my lad, as I did your father and grandfather before you; just say the word and your every wish will be granted!'

'Well, as you can probably appreciate, my small stature is a great problem; when it comes to the time of the year for the ploughing I am greatly handicapped. My brothers are able to plough acres of ground and get good crops, whilst I cannot reach to harness the horse or steady the shaft, let alone get my work done.'

'I fully sympathise with you, my son, and indeed I feel partly to blame. You see, when the mortals or so-called human beings first appeared on this planet – in a place called Eden I think it was, paradise, you know – and believe me it was a paradise till they came. They made a shambles of everything, trampling all before them, killing the animals, the fish and each other. We, of course, had to fly for our lives, we were no match for them, you see. Six times our size to start with; well, you know what I mean, being one of us.'

'No offence, sir, but just how do I happen to be one of you?' said Camisutory.

'Well, it was your great-grandfather, and all due respect, he was a freak of a fellow; likeable enough when he was young but as he grew, getting bigger and bigger, trampling us wee folk under his feet, there just wasn't room for him. And I took him, I left him outside one night. We seldom go out except at night, but I felt sure he would be all right in the hands of Màiri Bhàn, your great-grandmother, an immense mortal who used to draw water at the well out there (she was always bleating and wishing for a son, anyway). Well, he in turn got married to a mortal himself and we were delighted to find his first born, your father, was one of us. We made great friends with him and he used to visit us nearly every night, till he got the pneumonia. Too bad. Had he taken my advice it would never have happened and he might have been alive today. Now, as to your own problems, you are very much mistaken in believing it is a handicap to be small; it is an advantage. The only thing that's wrong with you is your diet; you haven't got a scientific approach and you are poisoning yourself with mortal food, destroying your natural gifts! You can't see in the dark, you can't predict the future, you are constantly ailing and all because you take the wrong food and drink. All you want to do is to put two and two together, use your brains, your natural gifts! Unlike human beings we have the gift, the Gift of Knowledge; we are born with it and they have to acquire it. It was not always so, but nowadays their brains are clouded through the lack of ability to concentrate. You were never taught to concentrate, now were you? Never mind, we can soon put that right – it's like the tablet God gave to Moses; it would have been double-Dutch to him had he not had the Gift.

'Mortals travel too fast, they eat up their own energies, destroy their creative ability. Pause and think; there is no need to plough, to cook, to travel fast. You can grow crops, if it's crops you want, without ploughing, just use Paraquat to clear the ground, then sow the seed.'

'What is Paraquat?' asked Camisutory.

'Oh, Paraquat's a substance known to us that the mortals are barely aware of yet. Now you can feed yourself quite adequately with various mushrooms and fungi, algaes of different kinds, sea plankton, roots, plants, seaweeds, mussels, cockles and whelks, etcetera. You don't need much sleep either, if you know how to rest properly. Start by placing your feet to the North and your face to the East,' (and he gave a little demonstration on one of the stone slabs). 'Pacify your mind, then your body will take care of itself. Relax and remember, never drink heated water; it's not simple H_20 as the humans think, but a complicated pattern of polymers upset by boiling. It can do no possible good except for washing. Oh, and don't shelter from rain as you need it as much as the plants do; face the sun and the wind, as you need that too.

'Now, when everyone has everything they need provided for them by nature itself, there is no problem of strife and greed: everyone is happy and contented, as I hope you will be if you should decide to remain with us. Meanwhile,' said the Oracle, jumping up from his stone slab, 'you'll dine with us, of course, and I want you to meet my niece Talya, nicknamed Moony; you'll like her . . . I hope.' With that a large stone moved away from an inner cave and the space was mirrored by a creature of such exquisite shape and form Camisutory was instantly spellbound. He would never leave this place again, he knew, nor did he ever want to. Why should he? What have we to offer that could in any way compare?

No one ever goes down by the dyke where the weasels are now, for that's where they found his chanter, and sometimes at night you can hear a tune being played down there – which is funny, because the chanter is hanging as usual up on the kitchen wall.

Old New Year's Day

It was January the thirteenth, Old New Year's Day (or so they say in these parts); it was also my birthday.* The rugged north end of Skye was steeped in winter, its deep, eerie magic gripping one's soul. The early sun thrust defensive rays of light through the snow clouds, the patchy ice-blue sky streaked with silver was like the inside of a shell. The brave little snowdrops in my garden stretched their necks and raised their heads towards the morning. In a pensive, yet almost aggressive mood I thrust my cold feet into my wellington boots, hauled a scarf and duffle coat around me and made the first imprint of the day on the as yet uncleared, thick snow outside my back door.

Who wants a birthday anyway? God knows, I'd had enough of them, fifty-eight to be precise. If Kazik hadn't gone and died things might have been different. We might even have been happy here in this idyllic cottage, had he lived long enough to retire. Stiff and tense, I felt very old as I made my way up the hairpin bend towards the Staffin Road. The old road, not the coast road. I would leave that to the cars, lorries and vans that made walking almost impossible. Mind you, the scenic coast road had much to offer for tourism in the summer. There was Monkstadt House, where Flora MacDonald and her aunt gave shelter to the Bonnie Prince; Duntulm Castle, now in ruins (tut, tut to the Scottish Ancient Monuments Association) – no,

* This is a true story.

they could have it all. I knew it so well and was finished with it, finished with everything. I would turn right to the mountain road that led to the awesome Quiraing – this is what my ancestors would have done long ago. They turned and walked away leaving the young behind.

Tears rose in my eyes as I walked on and on past the storm-battered, drunken-looking telegraph poles that seemed to lurch towards me trailing their useless cables. There would be nine miles of this before I reached Staffin. I began to compose a half-Polish, half-Gaelic lament to the soul of my Kazik. The sound of my voice echoed and amplified in the mountains, gradually drifting away to an agonised wail . . . so what? No one could hear me, or could they? As I stared into the distance at the stark, rugged peaks of the sinister Quiraing, rivulets of snow and icicles dribbling from cleft ridges and cavities, like saliva from an old man's chin, I fancied I saw someone moving down the deep slope of the mountain – an eagle perhaps, or a fox – but, no, maybe not.

Some three miles further on to my immense surprise I came upon a tractor, of all things, half buried in the snow at the side of the road. And still deeper in the ditch I saw a trailer attached to it, with a large ram struggling fiercely to release itself from thick tethering ropes, bashing at the sides of the trailer with its magnificent curled horns. How on earth had it got there? This was madness! Who on earth could abandon a beast in such a way? Was it for the slaughter, or for the pot? If so, why couldn't they have killed it right away instead of letting it bash its brains out like this?

Half closing my eyes against the glare of the snow at this high altitude, I peered along the low ground and valleys hoping to see someone, anyone, and there he was – a figure, tall in the misty haze of the midday sun. He was carrying a shepherd's crook and appeared to be moving, rather, staggering towards me. But it was hard to tell as the snow was becoming patchy, lying like a white lace mantilla over the dark peaty ground. The man seemed to come and go, one moment approaching, the next moving away – was he real? Abraham, perhaps; the ram a sacrifice? This was ridiculous! I must shout to him, let him know in no uncertain terms what I think of his treatment of this poor beast.

'Hey, you there! Here a minute!' but there was no reply – only the echo of my own voice, or was it God's?

A sound singing in my ears, drifting eerily around and above me, 'A-bra-ham . . . Ab-ra-ham . . . release the ram, the woman is the sacrifice . . . release the ram-am-am . . .'

'Release that damn ram, you abominable snowman!' I yelled. Then, ignoring my lapse into fantasy I pulled myself together, for it was obvious he could not hear me. I must try to get nearer, try to catch up with this inhuman freak. Good job I was wearing my wellies – I would have to leave the road to pursue him, but the more I rushed and stumbled towards him, sliding on ice-covered peat-bogs, grabbing at frozen reeds and banging my shins on snowy granite boulders, the further away he seemed to get. I tried shouting in Gaelic – that should get him! But it had no effect.

Utterly exhausted now and becoming more and more angry, I forced my breath and yelled at the top of my voice. I felt sure he could hear me full well, but he still ignored me. What a bastard! For all he knows I might be ill, lost, pregnant, mad – why the hell doesn't he answer? I took a quick look back and realised I had lost sight of the road. I had lost my bearings, now also sight of the man – 'Mother of God, I am lost!' I must look for a river; that was the thing to do. The Conon or the River Rha would flow towards the sea. What a son of a bitch the man was to leave a distressed woman a good eleven miles from anywhere, let alone a tied-up ram! And now the mist was coming down – it would be dark by four o'clock this time of year. I might have to stand still, till someone finds me, or stay there till morning. But it was not the dreaded mist that I could see after all, it was new smoke – there must be a house somewhere near.

Like someone stalking a stag, I stealthily made my way towards where there must surely be a dwelling. I could hear the sound of the river now, guessed it to be the Rha. It was a very dangerous river indeed, flowing deep into the ravine. To fall in would be certain death, but, fortunately for me, there was a flicker of light. It was from a cottage window. My mystery man must have arrived there! I drew as close as I dared, I would not knock or enter until I could see for myself the lie of the land. I hid down behind an old cart, watching, listening, my heart pounding fit to burst. I could hear agitated voices, men's and women's. Then two men came through the door, started to build a fire at the side of the house, feeding it with piles of rubbish, pulling out pieces of flaming rag from time to time, waving them, causing a revolting acrid smell. Then they returned inside, slamming the door behind them. Now was my chance, I would creep up and keek through the window.

As I got closer I could hear wailing and crying, Gaelic dirges being sung. It must be some kind of ritual or wake; had they caught that wretched ram to sacrifice it to the Moon? A' gheallaidh – moon-worshippers – that's it! I had heard there were still very strange practices going on around Staffin; it was, after all, the very last place in Skye to convert from paganism to Christianity (they didn't even have wee Frees for long enough). Wasn't it a child from hereabouts that the notorious Maighstir Ruairidh, Minister of Kensaleyre, re-fused to christen because its parents were pagan, sinners in his eyes? For five or more years he created a rumpus at the

Church of Scotland Assembly in Edinburgh, finally seeing the light and having the child christened after all.

On my hands and knees I crawled right up to the window. The men were silent now, there was no noise except for the moaning of the two women huddled in the middle of the floor, their heads and faces covered in black knitted shawls, grotesque shadows on the wall behind them caused by the dim light of the spluttering candles. One man was sitting by a table, his arms stretched across the whole length of it, wrists dangling limply over the side, his black, curly head fallen between his arms (reminding me somewhat of Salvador Dali's painting *The Hanging Christ*). Was this man meant for the sacrifice, or was he dead already? The other man bobbed jerkily up and down around the skirting board splashing liquid from a dark green bottle, showering everything in the room, including the women. Was it some kind of potent incense, holy water even? What I was seeing put the fear of death in me, froze my spine. What if they saw me, caught me? I would most surely be their next victim.

Creeping stealthily away I then leapt to a large tree, its naked branches scraped clean by the wild hens, squatting like sinister black crows in this spooky half-light. The trunk of the tree was sufficient to hide me meanwhile, until I could make my escape and try to get home – or be forever damned. I would certainly not go in there now, that's for sure! So, I made towards the river, looking back over my shoulder now and then to see if I was being followed. The moon was full, and I could see more clearly to pick my way with care and trepidation.

Suddenly, there was a loud grating noise; it was both sides of the cottage door being shoved open (they seldom opened both left and right sides, except for coffins and furniture – but it was neither). The older man was staggering out with a long, white bundle over his shoulder, six feet long, if an inch! My God! They must have killed the other fellow! I lay flat, deep in the snow, far too terrified to even feel the cold. I was completely numb, useless, watching that strong brute of a man carry his human sacrifice to the river and dump it, unceremoniously, as though it were a sack of whelks. Down, down, into the deep gully, causing a delayed, horrific, loud splash as it entered the depths of the dark brown mountain pool. They'd really done him in! Holy Mother of God, I'd seen it all! Immediately, the beast of a man had made his way back and closed the door behind him.

I ran for it, hell for leather, blindly tumbling, falling, rolling down the banks of the river, having enough of my senses left to keep a good margin between myself and its treacherous roaring falls. It was nine o'clock at night when I got home, wondered why the house was all lit up? Of course it would be, it was my birthday! I had forgotten there was to be a party, more of a céilidh really, just a few local friends and my sister.

It was she who opened the door and blasted on me, 'Where the hell have you been? You look a sight! Have you forgotten it's your birthday? We've all started. Morag and Farquhar can't wait long, you see, on account of the baby. Andy the Loon is here too.'

'Oh, hello, Seadan!' I cut in, embracing the local postman and taking the glass from his hand. 'Get yourself another!'

After two toddies and a hot bath I felt human again, and with much embellishment, as is my wont, I recounted my adventures. They believed me – every word of it! Farquhar even said he knew the shepherd, 'a fool of a fellow, wandering about in the hills till the pubs open – a roaring alcoholic, of course!'

I thought to myself, 'You can talk!'

Morag said, 'It was the Black Art; they've been flinging bodies in the River Rha for years, to say nothing of the sheep!'

Ach, what was the use? My best plan was to sleep on it – heaven knows I was tired beyond belief. I would ring Doctor Munro in the morning and get his advice, maybe get him to report it to the police, if he thought it the right thing to do.

'Is that you, Calum?' I said, and started to tell him about the day before, how it had all begun, the weeping, the depression and all.

'What the hell is the meaning of ringing me up at this time in the morning to complain about the symptoms of the menopause, woman?' he bellowed. But when I told him the rest of it he started to roar with laughter, then stopped abruptly. 'It's no laughing matter,' he said, 'I was up there myself two days ago putting the sheet over Old Angus Stalker – he's dead, you know. Keep it to yourself, though, don't want the whole place panicking. The less people know about it the better. It was diphtheria, you know, mighty contagious; that's why I told them to burn all his clothes and fumigate the house. They are very poor, you know, they wouldn't have had enough paraffin to burn up the mattress: trust them to roll it up and chuck it in the river! As if I don't have enough to do already, without having all the water supply polluted. As for fumigating, his brother Donald John must have been using uisge-beatha (whisky, the water of life). It's the only kind of fumigation they know about in these parts. As for holy water, it must have been his son Eachan coming home with it, he's probably got a whisky still somewhere up in the Quiraing – no wonder he didn't want to speak to you! Salvador Dali, indeed! Dead drunk, more like it. It's a wonder he wasn't under the table rather than over it! What an ordeal you've had, lassie; would you like me to prescribe you some pills? These weeping bouts of yours can't last long with your temperament . . . what about the flushes now?'

'Oh, shut up, Calum!' Come on over this evening and tell me why they tethered the ram.'

'Ach, come on! Aren't you a bit long in the tooth to be needing a lecture on the birds and the bees?' he said, 'but I'll try to come over.'

Meanwhile, there was a loud knocking at the back door. I opened it and saw to my astonishment a huge, black, glass-sided hearse; Charlie Smith, the undertaker, standing there grinning (a nice lad, I knew his father well).

'What the hell do you think you're doing with that contraption here?' I said. 'Everyone will think I've died. You'd better come inside and wait!'

'It will be a dickens of a long wait, then,' he said, 'you look as fit as a fiddle and as young as ever!'

'Don't be daft!' I muttered.

'I can't stay just now anyway, I'm on my way to Staffin to collect a corpse (Old Angus Stalker), but I'll call on my way back for a cup of tea.'

'You'll do no such thing! If you think I'm going to make tea for you and a corpse, you've got another think coming! Away with you, lad, anyway, you're far too late,' I shouted after him. 'They gave that corpse up as a sacrifice to the Moon God (A' ghealach) last night. I was at the ceremony myself!' And I watched the old glass hearse accelerating on the hairpin bend up the steep incline to Staffin.

Doctor Munro was in good form that night. He sang for my sister and myself and told many stories, but the funniest of all was his explanation of the tupping of the rams. 'It's a sort of family planning, you understand. If they can't do it to us, at least they can try it on the rams! The tupping season is over in January, round about now. In a climate like ours you can't have the lambs born too early in the spring – they'd perish! Of course, it's the reverse procedure at the end of November. You must have seen those sheep in Lewis and Harris – maybe you thought they were prisoners of war? The ones with the colourful patches stitched on their posteriors? Well, the farmers remove those when the tupping season begins . . . for obvious reasons, you understand! Oh, by the way, I was down at the pier to see if I could get some prawns, and Cally Murchison's boat came in.

'Have you time for a quick one, Doctor?' Cally had asked, 'I'm needing one badly myself. I nearly had a bad turn there. I thought I saw a human corpse come floating towards the boat, out there in the middle of the bay. I gaffed it and hauled it on board, cutting the ropes. I can tell you I was scared stiff! When, would you believe it, out rolled a blooming mattress! Some joker needs his head seeing to! Why didn't they just burn the damn thing, instead of causing a hazard to navigation?'

'Ach well, Cally m'boy – just you put it all down to experience!' said Calum Munro the doctor.

'Slàinte mhór!'*

---

* Slàinte mhór! – A toast to your great health!

The Wrath of God

This year the Highlands and Islands received a vibrating shock – the murder in Lewis of an elderly woman living alone! Who would believe it? There had been no such thing for more than two hundred years and a great deal of distress was caused by the questioning of innocent neighbouring families. Mind you, many of the stories one hears at a céilidh in Skye (for instance) reveal that there could have been one or two people knocked off during and before that time, but the blame was always conveniently placed on the head of a ban-sìth, a water kelpie, or some such strange phenomenon.

I am not saying that this is a true story I am going to tell you; but I just want to give you an idea of the sort of thing that could go on, was believed and became legend . . .

There were two old cailleachs once living in Uig – or rather, the one lived in Idrigill and the other in Cuil. Their crofts were facing each other across the bay and there was hardly a day that would pass but you would see one or other of them trotting round the shore road with bits of gossip, new-laid eggs or rhubarb jam to give to each other. They were very pally, you see. Mind you, all this activity created a problem for Seadan (the Post) who never knew which home they were staying in. If he delivered the post at Idrigill, Beathag was sure to be at Cuil; and, if he took the trouble of climbing all the way down the Brae at Cuil, Cairistiona would like as not be over in Idrigill.

Now, these two sisters had yet another sister who had

married a sailor and gone over to New Zealand to live. She had a large family and her husband had taken to farming instead of to the sea, and they had prospered through the years. They never forgot to write regularly to the two widowed sisters back home. Now this regular mail from New Zealand raised the curiosity of a certain young crofter – a ne'er-do-well lout, good for nothing but scrounging on other people – and he took to watching the activities of the two old cailleachs very carefully. There wasn't a day but one or other of the houses was empty.

'What about taking a look inside?' he thought, the doors in the Highlands never being locked, summer or winter. And this was the month of March – the middle of March – the time for the falaisgairs: the burning of the heather and rubble so that the new grass can grow unhindered to feed the sheep and cattle. The children would prance round from door to door beseeching permission to set the croft on fire. They usually got the go-ahead, with the warning not to burn all the fences – but not from Beathag and Cairistiona. They were far too soft-hearted and sorry for the nesting birds, mice, moles and voles – so terrified they sometimes came into the house. It is a pathetic sight to see a bundle of terrified rabbits perched on the very edge of a granite rock, with an inferno of heather burning around them, so they never gave permission.

Well, one crisp, late afternoon when the sun was setting golden in the sky Cairistiona walked round to see Beathag at Idrigill. While she was gone, evil got the better of Murdo the Crooked One, and he sneaked into the house at Cuil, started ransacking the place looking for New Zealand letters in which he hoped to find who knows what? Money, perhaps! In his eagerness he had not shut the back door behind him. When Seadan with the late mail, saw it open from the top of the croft, he presumed that Cairistiona would be at home so, swearing and cursing as was his usual, he lumbered down the croft and walked in, quite the thing. And being a big, brave burly Highlander, when he saw the caper Murdo was up to, clobbered the daylights out of him, leaving him a sorry-looking sight, and turned to leave the house. But Murdo was a sneak and not nearly as hurt as he pretended – so, when he got Seadan's back turned, he ups and bashes him over the head with the heavy iron tongs from the fireplace. The poor postman fell to the floor dead as mutton. (It was murder, all right!)

That night as Cairistiona made her way home across the sandy bay, the tide being well out and the moon already at the half, she was astonished to see that her croft was on fire. 'Mhic an Sad!'* she said to herself. 'Just wait till I get a hold of these amadans. Never before did anyone burn my croft and without my permission.' But that was not all, by a long shot. When she reached her cottage she found it had been ransacked – the dresser-drawer in the kitchen all spilt out on the floor, the bowls and milk jugs smashed and the tongs lying in the middle of the room. She almost had a bad turn, feeling faint and sick.

In the next few days Cairistiona and her sister combed the district from end to end looking for the culprits but no one knew anything – they even denied lighting the falaisgair. But the funny thing was that Seadan the Post was missing. The most honourable man in the district and well beloved, he hadn't delivered a single letter for more than three days and his wife was nearly demented. She got the police from Portree and no one could find sight nor sound of him, till, one day, weeks after, Cairistiona went to put her favourite goat into an old roofless bochan on her croft.

There would be sweet grass grazing in there and the falaisgair wouldn't have reached it; but, when she got inside

* Mhic an Sad – Son of the Devil

she got the shock of her life! Instead of the grass and nettles she expected, she found the charred body of Seadan burnt beyond all recognition. The local verdict was, of course, that he had gone in there to relieve himself, that the falaisgair had reached him before he had time to get out. No one ever knew or suspected that he might have been dragged there deliberately. No one, that is, save Murdo who had since gone out of his mind or 'mach as a rian', as they say in the Gaelic; but that didn't surprise anyone either since his auntie and his sister had gone the same way. So, there was no one to point the finger at the wretched man and no punishment either – save for the wrath of God.

Hairy Lady

This story begins in Edinburgh. The young man paced about restlessly from one side of the room to the other, opening drawers, pulling out shirts and socks, turning over photographs, opening the windows. The day was hot; removing his tie and undoing the buttons at his neck, he went to get a cool drink from the fridge. At least she couldn't have the fridge – that was his, and all its contents. Seòras had decided finally to separate from his live-in girlfriend.

They had been going together for about three years and quite by accident Seòras had discovered, listening to conversation in the pub the other night, that she had gone off with a fellow he knew and disliked intensely; whereas she had told him that she was going on a couple of weeks' holiday with her poor old aunt – who couldn't travel alone any more because she was partially blind, needed someone to fiddle about with tickets and so on. She was most convincing about the whole thing. So when Seòras found out the truth he was absolutely shattered; although he was fed up with her anyway, she had some horrid little habits, biting her nails, fiddling with her hair; she was always using dye that stank, made the bathroom smell horrid. Things like that were really getting his goat. Finally he had put it to her that he knew what she had been up to, and she was furious – swore at him, threatened him, his job. But Seòras was determined now, this was the finish; he would have to get away from her, somehow.

So he had started to separate things, which would be hers

and which would be his, but of course in truth it was all his, since anything that was in the flat he had himself given to her as presents. However, she claimed everything and went off with a whole suitcase full of jewelry, ornaments and things which meant a great deal to Seòras in his time, had very rashly given her and now regretted it heartily. However, what are possessions after all?

He wondered and thought, 'Well, perhaps I had better take two or three weeks off work. I don't think they would mind at all. It's a good time of the year to do it. At least I've still got the car, so I'll make my way up to Skye where I was born and bred, where my beloved mother left me her house and croft. It is there standing empty and would need seeing to anyway. I'll take leave and at the same time do a bit of business. After all I am a sales representative, deal in plastic fish boxes and nautical gear. I can go round all the ports, do a little trading; at the same time I can relax, enjoy myself, try and recover from this horrific drama of a love-life gone wrong.' So poor Seòras drove steadily and doggedly north, telling himself not to look back, but to look ahead, think of the future, cast all these mistakes he had made out of his mind, and adjust himself to being a bachelor.

It was late that night before he got to the Isle of Skye. He had to continue once he had crossed the ferry to the north end. By the time he reached the vicinity of the old Staffin road where his house was it was late indeed. It was very eerie and strange walking into his mother's old croft house, standing empty for almost a year, seeing the ghosts and the shadows of his young days, the family all so happy there, his gay and wonderful mother cooking for them, amusing them, telling them stories. It all came back to him in a flood. He almost couldn't bear it any more. So he decided that he would walk for a while before going to bed. It was a bright night – in fact the moon hadn't arrived, the sun was still setting. And nothing could be more magnificent than the sunset coming down slowly behind the rocks, the mountains across the Sound, the waters of the Minch gleaming in a coat of many colours. The yellows, crimsons and purples that shone down upon the Minch were breathtakingly beautiful. It seemed to him like Jacob's coat of many colours – in fact he felt very much like Jacob must have done when he was abandoned by all his brothers and cast out to a foreign land.

Oh dear, he must really shake off this mood – so he chose to leave the main road, wander down a sheep track until he reached the shore, gleaming as it was with some multi-coloured and mainly white stones encircling the white sands, overlaid by seaweed lying gracefully, rather like Chinese moustaches draping an open mouth. He wasn't really concentrating on where he was going or what he was doing when he reached an outcrop of rocks; sinister, all black, with lots of caves and jutting-out bits – a sinister-looking place indeed. As he raised his head, lo and behold to his horror he saw something that he had never ever seen before – it absolutely terrified him.

Sitting in a cave was the most extraordinary creature he had ever seen – he couldn't make his mind up what it was, a gorilla, a yeti – but who in all their natural life had ever seen a yeti on the Isle of Skye? The mind boggled, and oh my God, there was smoke coming out of its nostrils, curling up towards the roof of the cave! Seòras didn't wait to see any more. He thought he must be going mad, over-tired, the strain of what he had been through over the last few weeks was too much for him. He would have to see a doctor. He turned on his heels and began to run. Which would be the best way to go? How could he escape from this thing? Run out into the sea, swim away – oh my God, he would die of cold! He was quite close to the Quiraing. He could scramble up one of those peaks, and if it came anywhere near him he could pelt it with stones and rocks from the top of the pinnacle. This was one idea.

But he just kept on running, out of breath and nearly fainting with fright, when he heard of all things a female voice calling to him shouting, 'Hey, don't be frightened, it's only skin deep! Please come back and I'll explain!'

Seòras stopped running, drew in his breath and said to himself, 'Well, it can't be all that ferocious if there's a female with it. It must be a keeper of some sort. I'd better go back a little way and see what I can see.' So, being in the kilt (he had changed as soon as he had reached the cottage – there is nothing like the freedom of the kilt especially when you are clambering amongst rocks, that is, if it's a night without midges) he drew his sgian dubh from the top of his stocking, cautiously made his way back, step by step, very, very slowly until he got to within a couple of yards of the creature. If it was a phantom there was nothing very much he could do about it. But if it was for real, he would have its guts for garters.

Becoming more and more brave every minute he said in a loud voice, 'What the hell are you?'

Whereupon the creature began to laugh loudly, and, as though scratching its head, put a claw up to its scalp, unzipped a zipper, thereby making the artificial skin (for that indeed is what it must have been) fall to its shoulders; and revealed to Seròas's astonishment quite the most beautiful head of hair he had seen for many years! A young childlike face, blue innocent eyes, snub nose and a cheery mouth cockily said to him, 'What the hell are you so scared about? It's only skin deep as I said.'

Whereupon Seòras took a couple of gigantic leaps and landed – plonk – beside her on the same rock in the cave. 'You scared the wits out of me,' he said. 'What's it all about? I've never seen a hairy woman before.'

'Oh,' she said, 'it's a commercial – we're doing a film, for toothpaste, you know. We're on location and the cameramen, the extras and everyone have all gone back to the hotel, but I wanted to stay here. I couldn't be bothered taking this ridiculous costume off; so I asked them to let me hold on to it – it's only a prop. Anyway, I wanted so badly to see the sun going down, I was really too tired to move.'

'Let me help you out of the rest of it,' said Seòras, observing she was wearing a t-shirt and jeans, looking quite respectable and unbelievably lovely. Her figure was slim, slightly tall and in every way rather enchanting. His luck was in. 'Look,' he said, 'don't you think you owe me a favour? After all you nearly gave me a heart attack and I am very lonely. I've only just arrived back in Skye. I wonder if you would be kind enough to have dinner with me down at my cottage. I have brought stuff from Marks & Spencers, deep freeze and that sort of thing, so there would be no cooking involved; and, I am really terribly lonely.'

'Gosh,' she said, 'I think I'll take you up on it. I am so bored with the camera crew and it would make a nice change. So hang on, I'll pick up all these bits and pieces and we can be off.'

So that evening the cottage came alive again. They chattered away merrily, lit candles, put on music and the heaters were on anyway. Seòras had seen to it that there was off-peak heating in his cottage, because nobody can keep a cottage in Skye without having it well aired and heated. They had a lot in common. Her parents were missionaries in China. They came over occasionally, but even when they were in this country they were so involved with politics and medicine, their own interests, that they hardly realised that they had a daughter. And as for Seòras, well, both his parents were dead.

'What about?' said Seòras, 'tomorrow and tomorrow and tomorrow, please, Griselda?' For that was her name, although he had made up his mind secretly that henceforth he would call her 'Grizzly' on account of the scare she had given him in her extraordinary grotesque attire.

'Well,' she answered, 'I am staying for a week and then the film will be finished; and I'll be out of a job.'

'Well,' said Seòras, 'that's just ideal. Maybe we can do something together. I'm up here to try and flog some of my marine equipment, fish containers and lobster creels, that sort of thing. I have got a boat, you know . . .'

'Boat,' she interrupted enthusiastically, 'my goodness, that would be marvellous. You know I heard of a fellow, he was a dentist, had a yacht, used to sail into all the ports all around France and Britain and through the canals. He had equipped his yacht as a dental surgery, carried as his crew three glamorous girls and had the time of his life.'

'Well, I can't quite rise to that,' said Seòras, 'but I could sail around with a Hebridean yeti and a boatload of creels, baskets and nautical equipment. You would be a great asset, you know, you would draw the crowds while I do the counting. How about it?'

So they made plans and told stories one after another and Seòras became happy again, voluble and told some quite amusing stories, one of which was about a friend of his, so he said. His name was Brahmaputra. He travelled much in foreign countries, in Africa and India. And one funny story when he was in Africa . . . he was a puny wee man, you know, with not much brawn or muscle, wandering away into the jungle – what did he come across but a big lion with great big teeth and an open mouth. Poor wee Brahmaputra didn't know what on earth to do. He had no weapons, no gun, nothing to defend himself, and couldn't run away fast enough – he knew that. So what he decided was to roll up his shirt sleeves and, clenching his fist, shove his arm right through the creature's open mouth, through its belly and its guts, till he reached the end of its tail. Then, with an immense tug, he pulled, and pulled its inside out! Then of course the lion could do nothing, and Brahmaputra made his escape.'

'What a load of rubbish you talk,' said Grizzly. 'And, by the way, I'd have you know I am not a Hebridean yeti, I happen to be a Himalayan bear, so there! Anyway, if we decide to use the hairy skin we would have to buy it off the film company.'

'Oh, don't worry,' said Seòras, 'I've plenty of money.'

Seòras worked very hard the next week, got his boat back on the water, all his cargo on board, a lot of printed pamphlets made, making a feature of the Hebridean yeti. And so not many weeks after that the pair of them set sail towards the rising sun. No doubt they would splice the main brace, and if not, tie the knot, or I'm a Dutchman!

And if you happen to be cruising in the Hebridean waters in the near future, don't be surprised if you see a small craft passing by with what looks like a baboon or a yeti sitting aft or for'ad, and probably a burly great Highlander steering, singing as he goes, one of his old ditties that he must have learned years ago when he was young:

> I went to the animal fair
> All the birds and the beasts were there
> The gay baboon in the light of the moon
> Was combing his auburn hair
> The monkey slid out of his bunk
> And slid down the elephant's trunk
> The elephant sneezed and fell to his knees
> So what became of the monkey, monkey, monk?

And off they go, sailing merrily away!

Nothing Leads to Nowhere

That's what I said when I confronted the cattle gate high up in the hills above Glen Conon. It was too hot a day for walking really, but since I had got a lift as far as this, since there was no longer a proper road, I decided to explore along a peat track. I would be all right, surely, so long as I kept my eye on the River Conon that flowed back down to Uig where I lived. The trouble was I was keeping my eye on the wrong river, possibly the River Rha. Rivers have always intrigued me, and it occurred to me suddenly that I had never ever followed one right the way up, to discover its source. It was an exciting idea.

So I opened the cattle gate to a new, remote, unbelievably beautiful world, a vast basin of wild peaty moss-grown earth, walled by mini-mountains, studded with glittering waterfalls. Behind me far below lay Uig, the Ascrib Islands and Waternish Point. Soon the peat track was no more; it had ended abruptly where the peats had once been cut, dried and gathered. 'Was that all I had come to find? Nonsense, nothing never leads to nowhere,' I said. Besides, people had obviously lived here once; why, further up beside the river was what looked like a community centre, whole heaps of houses buried under short grass dotted only with white daisies. I danced on the top of one of them. Twirling round and round I realised it must have been a sort of fortress or broch. You could see for miles, far away and over the sea. And look, close by and in the river were great hunks of smooth flat stones where the women must have done their washing. I imagined I saw one of them;

it was Màiri Bhàn, for sure. She waved to me, and I waved back (it didn't matter that she wasn't there).

Then I continued, following this knobbly unpredictable river closely. It was doing strange things: splitting in places, chasing round pieces of land forming miniature islands, leaving behind it a surf of frothy white like lace; then joining together again into endlessly deep brown pools, fed by water-falls that streaked down shimmering rocks with ferns and wild flowers dripping from its flow. And the music, oh, the music! Everything from harmonious tinkling drips to grand queru-lous growls; then, surprisingly, the river disappeared com-pletely underneath a mossy pile of earth. But not the sound – its music continued underneath my feet, a swift wild torrent gurgling and spluttering beneath me. And look! There was another and another; tiny little rivers all going nowhere. It can't be; no, no, I would have to follow the big one.

I leapt along beside it from heather hunk to heather hunk and boulder to boulder. It wasn't so easy any more, I was getting out of breath. It was also a lot colder, so I pulled down the sleeves of my jumper. I knew nothing of time and cared less. Perhaps some of my ancestors had been explorers (my grandfather had sailed the seas, it's true). Look again, sub-merged houses by this deep pool – another Skara Brae? To lie here on this short grass sheltered by half submerged walls put up before the living memory of man – how I wished I could go on a dig.

Meanwhile the river was calling again, booming out from under the earth, the ground getting increasingly dangerous. Great pitch-black scabs of peat marred the earth where some disturbance had flung great chunks high into the air. There they stood like giant Negroes with scorched and tufted heather hair. And the river? Why the river had gone. The little that remained had seeped into the black peat, was babbling up here and there in the form of tiny pools, and further over there were bigger lochs, black as sin.

Then I looked around more generally. I had followed my river and knew its source, but now, where was I? I was lost. My God, the Quiraing! I had reached the Quiraing without knowing it – the most awe-inspiring, chewed-up outcrop of rocks on the whole of Skye. What was I doing here? How did I get here? What's beyond that fence? No, no, it can't be; a sheer drop of thousands of feet to – yes, that was Staffin, and I was high on the top of the mountains. I was a flippin' mountaineer without even knowing it! Over there I could see the Seven Sisters' red point, and even Loch Torridon. It was magnificent. Beneath me all the houses in Staffin and several not so small lochs, and I was up here all alone amongst the craigs and peaks – what was the mountain to my right, though? I couldn't quite see the top of it for the rolling mist.

The mist – was I mad? The sooner I got out of here the better. I had forgotten all about the mist, the number of people who had been caught in it and died right here, just where I was standing. Sure enough, it was swirling down towards me at a hell of a lick. I must keep calm, find the river again, and quickly. Even if I couldn't see it I could hear it, must listen for that gurgling noise, it should lead me back the way I came. I began to run, jump, tumble down the mountain, leaping and jumping and steeling myself against fear and panic. I could see the black peat men again. The river was showing up here and there, but the mist was moving nearer and nearer. Faster and faster I urged myself; I took an extra long leap, coming slap down with my leg twisted beneath me – I knew no greater agony. It was excruciating, I was passing out. I daren't, I simply dare not pass out here, miles from anywhere. No one would ever find me, no one; the pain was intolerable, I was sunk, finished.

I prayed with all my heart, remembered how the footballers on television always forced themselves up again. If they could do it I could; I'd have to, I didn't want to be found dead. Think of what it would cost looking for me – long lines of yellow-clad mountain rescue teams, a sinister helicopter hovering overhead and me unable to shout or be heard. Anyway I wasn't worth it; I wasn't worth a twopenny piece. Damn the way I felt right now – come on, try! And I tried dragging myself along sideways, then managed to get up and hop, stumble, roll, tumble, down the side of the river till I came at last, tears streaming down my face, to the gate that had led to nowhere.

It was lucky for me, the shearing was on in Glen Conon that same evening and all the local men were working late. A dutiful and kindly wife had brought them tea. She had it in a big square breadbasket under a red and white cloth, oatcakes and cheese. The oatcake was out of this world; coarse, succulent, delicious. I ate and drank in a sort of trance gratefully. I sat and watched a small boy slash a streak of blue paint on the backsides of his father's sheep – so as to know one from the other, I supposed. At any rate I was glad they didn't sneck their ears. I had pain enough of my own, heaven knows, without witnessing more.

I listened to the warnings and wise 'might-have-beens' from a blue-eyed elderly bodach, but eternally young man, who sat on the dyke rolling a cigarette or cutting tobacco. I was too far through to know which. I could hear his voice as they got me to a car – 'Think of all those helicopters searching for you, and not so long ago there was a young fellow, a foreigner he was. Three whole days before they got him. He was dead of course, dead as mutton. Dead as mut . . .'

Yes, they'd had to send for the doctor that same night. It wasn't so much the sprained ankle as the emotional and physical strain that made me conk out on them.

'What the devil were you doing up there anyway?' said the doctor when I regained consciousness. 'You might have been killed, do you not know that, woman?'

'Yes, I know it now,' I said, 'but I also know that nothing leads to nowhere, and what a river looks like at its source.'

Four Fingers

Jock was expert at sharpening the scythe. 'There's an art in it,' he said. In fact, he was better at sharpening the scythe than he was at cutting the grass. It's true the exercise kept his weight down, the swaying motion and rippling waves in the long grass made him think he was back at sea again. Nevertheless, it was exhausting work. Every now and then he found it necessary to sit for a while on the dyke to take a breather, fill his pipe, cutting the black twist tobacco lovingly in the palm of his hand, and keeping an eye out too, for his son Calum.

It was Calum who usually brought him his dinner, that is, if he had no other ploy on. He was a rascal for disappearing if there was any work to do. But here he was at last, running towards his father hell for leather and no basket – empty-handed, not even the red spotted hankie with the scones and crowdie in it. He didn't seem to have so much as a can of meal and water.

'What on earth is wrong . . . where's my dinner?' said Jock.

'I gave it to a man, father, a stranger,' Calum panted out. 'I think he's ill. I found him lying face down on the shore, and I dragged him into Charlie's Cave and left him there, with the food. He is a queer kind of creature, I couldn't make head nor tail of him.'

'Was he off a boat?' put in Jock.

'I don't know, it's a mystery; he was just lying there, couldn't seem to utter a word – either in English or Gaelic.'

'Charlie's Cave did you say? Is that where you put him?

Come on then, we may as well take a dander down and see
what it is you're blethering about.' He leant his scythe against
the dyke tenderly, its sword-sharp edge gleaming in the sun.
'Wait . . . wait a minute, lad . . . not so fast!'

But Calum didn't answer, for he was off now, making for
the rocks down by the sea. It was heavy going for Jock, being
kind of corpulent, so he soon fell far behind, decided to give
up the ploy altogether and thrash that young rascal when he
got him home. He was just about to turn back when he came
on a rugged outcrop of rocks which partly concealed a stretch
of white sand. There, glittering on the edge of the sand was
the most extraordinary object he had ever seen . . . it looked as
if it were made of crystal, reflecting light all round it. Jock
didn't know whether it was a boat or a plane . . . or what? And
there was his son Calum standing beside it, apparently talking
to what looked like a man dressed in a sort of armour.

Jock felt a queer sensation down his back as the fear of death
crept over him; he yelled to his son to come back at once, for
he knew he must be in imminent danger. He thought he saw
the man take hold of his son's hand, then they withdrew from
each other sharply. With intense relief he saw the man get
into the machine and suddenly, silently, become airborne.

Jock waited till the queer object was well out of sight.
Calum was walking back now, along the edge of the tide, his
hands in his pockets, his head hanging low: 'So well he might,'
thought Jock, 'this will take a bit of explaining.'

But Calum refused to explain anything; all he would say
was, 'I don't know, I don't know who the man was, or what
kind of a plane it was . . . I only saw the thing myself just
now . . . it wasn't there when I found the man . . . if indeed he
was a man. He never uttered a single word all the time he was
here . . . just made queer sounds. I tried to get him to come
home with me, but he kept shying away as though he was

terrified; so making signs and beckoning to him, I led him up to Charlie's Cave till I would get you. That was this morning when I took your dinner and left it with him. I took him some water from the well too; but all the time he was listening and watching the sky from the mouth of the cave. After a bit he smiled at me. And now, when that queer thing came out of the sky, he came and tried to touch me, then drew his arm away quick as though I were made of fire. Then, as you saw for yourself, he was gone.'

'Well, listen Calum,' said Jock, 'not a word of all this to anyone; it will need proper investigation. They would only think we were barmy if we told anyone. There's been enough queer things going on in this island lately, heaven knows, what with lights flashing off and on up at the quarry.'

'Yes, and that car that's been seen even in daylight,' said Calum.

'What car?'

'The one they've seen coming along with its lights on, when they drive into the side of the road to let it past, it doesn't come forward . . . it isn't there.'

'Oh! Man, man,' said Jock, 'that's a terrible bad omen. Worse than the blood on the stairs that Maggie Creasdean saw, the same day that her brother was murdered in Toronto. Come on home, boy, I'm getting the creeps.'

'And . . . wait a bit,' said Calum, as they started walking briskly away. 'There was that old pilgrim preacher cycling home one dark night past the graveyard when he felt hands pulling at his morning coat. When he got off his bicycle in a cold sweat, he found that it was just the lining of his coat caught in the spokes; every time the wheels went round they gave a sort of jerk . . . do you think it's going to be the end of the world, father?'

But before Jock could answer they were home again. That same evening Jock went back down to the shore again, on his own, to look around. There must be an explanation; of all the happenings he had ever heard of, this was the strangest. He wanted to make sure that he had seen what he had seen. So, he looked for tracks and footsteps; they were there all right, Calum's and his own, and the immense footprints of the stranger.

He took a look in the so-called Charlie's Cave and, sure enough, there was the red spotted handkerchief, with the food still in it. Then, moving his torch all round him he found lying in the shadows (no doubt overlooked by the man in his hurried departure) what looked like a glove, only instead of having five fingers, it had only four, and they were facing each other like lobsters' claws, or maybe sugar tongs. Jock felt sick, uneasy, and began to shiver. He felt that he and his son had stumbled on something uncanny, far beyond their ken; maybe it would be as well to tell the minister, or maybe the policeman after all.

But there was no need, for early next day a stranger arrived in the village. He said he was a newspaper reporter, but Jock felt sure he was not; he was more like one of those Tory MPs that come up for the elections.

'Can you tell me about any strange happenings on the island lately, Jock?' he said. 'I hear you are a bit of an authority on strange phenomena.'

'I don't know what you're talking about,' said Jock, 'unless it's a new kind of cattle food you're trying to sell me. I am, as fine you know, a farmer.'

'No offence, old fellow, but we just wondered if you had seen by any chance anything strange or unusual – oh, come on man, a helicopter maybe?'

'Is that what it was?' said Jock, standing on one leg and slicing away at the black twist; he enjoyed keeping this Sassenach fellow dangling for a bit. Nevertheless, he intended

to tell him all he knew, for he seemed like a man of con-
sequence and obviously knew something about the strange
craft already. But you should have seen his face when Jock
showed him the glove; he was flabbergasted.

'You will of course let me have it, won't you, Jock?' he
beseeched.

'Well, I'm not so sure; I kind of fancy it myself as a sort of
souvenir.'

'I can quite understand that,' said the man, 'but confiden-
tially I have been commissioned to give you quite a sum of
money should you care to collaborate with me. Your information is of vital importance to our country . . .'

'And you are no newspaper man,' said Jock, looking him in
the eye.

'Well, no; I see we are beginning to understand each other.
What would you say to fifty pounds?'

And Jock went on cutting his tobacco.

'It's your money, man, yours and your son's.'

'Well, as a matter of fact, I badly need a new tractor.'

'A tractor it is then, a silent tractor . . . not a word to anyone
about this whole affair. You can vouch for your son?'

'Well, he's young – I can't guarantee . . .'

'Has he got a bicycle?' the man broke in.

'No,' said Jock.

'Well, I'm sure he could do with one for going to school.'

'Right enough,' said Jock, 'and I'm sure yourself could be
doing with a cup of tea!'

Towards the end of that same summer, when the corn was
early in (largely through the help of the new tractor) and the
days were getting shorter, the nights longer, Jock roasted his
feet at the fire. Calum sat doing his homework (by his own
way of it). In fact, he sat spinning a small round flat disc in the
lamp light.

'Give me that thing and get on with your work, for heaven's sake,' said Jock snatching the disc as it fell.

'No, no, please, father, it's mine, the man gave it to me!'

Jock stared at the object that lay in his hand. Amazed, fascinated by the four little lights that moved round and round on the surface of the slim disc. Slowly, he raised his head and looked Calum full in the eyes: 'What man, Calum?'

'Why the man from space, father, of course.'

The Broken Daisy Chain

Some people think that living in the Isle of Skye must be one long picnic. It's true that men and women all mucked in while working on the crofts at the peats with a basket of bannocks and a can of buttermilk. But nowadays the women are mostly tied indoors catering for bed-and-breakfast, making up sandwiches in cellophane for tourists to take away with them, or giving the schoolchildren packed meals for taking on charity walks – there is little time for picnics, as such.

Nevertheless, one very hot summer, when I was a girl of sixteen, my mother, who had a mania for looking at houses for sale (and buying them too, if she got away with it) suggested that we all go on a picnic to the north end of the island. 'There was an old manse somewhere near Kensaleyre in very bad repair,' she said, 'and it might go cheap.' (My father showed no interest whatsoever.) So, Doctor Nicholson, a very good friend of the family, offered to take us in his car.*

I was keen to go: whereas my mother wanted to buy houses, I wanted to paint them. I persisted relentlessly in making amateurish sketches of whitewashed cottages with brown peat stacks leaning up against their gable ends, or cailleachs feeding chickens at their front porches; most of them ended up in a cupboard under the stairs, or were exhibited briefly in the bathroom, to be removed hurriedly if we expected guests. One often hears of people who have one persistent dream.

* This story is absolutely true.

Well, for as long as I can remember, I had dreamt about a large tumbledown house with a protruding porch on bleak high walls – but I had never tried to make a sketch of it till the day before the picnic.

After helping mother fill the thermos flasks, and carrying the baskets to the car, I ran back impulsively for my paints. I selected some colours, then looked around for a hogs-hair brush and some white. The doctor was blowing the horn impatiently, but somehow or other I knew I simply must take white paint with me. When I had found it I ran down the gravel path, climbed into the car and we were off.

I adored the doctor, who was twice my age, a bachelor and very shy – it was great fun teasing him. And, as a half-native of Skye, I was too used to the scenery to enthuse about it. I just knew that I found the island better than anywhere else in the wide world.

After leaving Broadford our first stop was Portree, the handful of shops in Wentworth Street thrilled me more at that silly age than all the Cuillins put together. When we eventually found the old manse my mother was so keen about, I stopped dead, staring open-mouthed at the overgrown glebe, the moss-grown path, the tall pines casting sinister shadows across the protruding porch. 'It's my dream!' I shouted.

'It is rather nice!' said Mother.

'No! You don't understand. I know this place. I've been here before.' And I started peering through the large flat six-pane windows, then ran round the back while the doctor and my mother entered by the front door respectfully, having got the key from the solicitor in Portree.

I found the fish box at the foot of the scullery window, where it had always been, slid and loosened the broken sneck on the window with a firm jerk, as I had always done. Climbing in, I went straight to the kitchen. It was just the same. I looked under the primitive sink for the pipe clay, but it had gone. Then I opened my satchel and got to work.

When my mother reached the kitchen, she found me on my knees painting a daisy chain round the edge of the cement floor. 'What on earth do you think you're doing?' she said.

'Well! I had to finish it. The pattern was only half-way round.'

'Let's get out of here!' said the doctor, 'the place gives me the creeps!'

We were all very silent on the way home. I was very sleepy, but we had to stop in Portree to return the key to the solicitor, and my mother insisted on going in alone. It wasn't until the following spring, when we were doing out the cupboard under the stairs and my sketch of the manse turned up, that my mother told the story she had managed to extract from the very reluctant solicitor.

'It's funny you should have drawn this sketch the day before you saw the manse,' she said. 'I think we will just burn it. It's so sad and eerie, it frightens me so much . . . to think that you finished painting the daisy chain that that poor kitchen-maid was making when she was murdered!'

'What on earth are you talking about?'

'Yes!' continued Mother. 'Long ago that was a wealthy parish; the manse was well appointed with good silver and gifts from the parishioners. A couple of hooligans from the mainland got to know that the offertory was kept there for several weeks, before the minister (who was old) could get it sent away. So they thought they would get a good haul there, break in through the back window when they thought the servants were out. But there happened to be a new young scullery-maid at the time and she was so eager to please. She stayed up late one night, making patterns round the kitchen floor with pipe clay. And when the burglars came in on her she screamed and they ran off – but not before they had struck her on the head so hard that it killed her. They got away too, but they say her ghost was often seen after that. There were never any offers for the place so they pulled it down. Small wonder! They should have done it years ago.'

'Well, they couldn't till I had finished the daisy chain, could they?'

'Uist, uist!'* said my mother in Gaelic, as she quickly made off with my ill-fated sketch.

* Uist, uist! – Don't say such things!

Jacob's Ladder

The old American rocking-chair squelched and groaned as it bent backwards and forwards on its rusty springs. 'But it looked very nice,' thought Morag; after all, she had taken great pains to strip it, and cover the back and seat in white sheepskins.

Morag Fletcher, you see, was a very trendy young woman, and stripped wood was all the go at the time. She didn't have the facilities on this remote island that she would have had in Glasgow or London, but she was never stuck. Though it was with some astonishment that the local fishermen noticed a rocking chair and a couple of carved pedestals tied on a rope to the end of the pier: 'To be bleached,' Morag explained, 'by the salt water and the sea air.' And there's no doubt about it, they thought she was plain daft.

'Do you think you could ask Annie to find some oil to put on the springs of this chair, darling?' said her mother one evening, giving her knitting wool an irritable little tug with her pinky. 'The grating is driving me slowly mad.'

'It's Annie's night off, mother, she's gone to the dance in the hall.'

'Oh yes, I'd forgotten. I do hope she won't be late again . . . shussh . . . what was that? Was that a knock at the door?'

'Ach, mother, you're always so jumpy when father's away. I didn't hear anything . . . wait a bit, though, it sounds like a car. I'll have a look.'

Soon there was a crunch on the gravel, and a loud banging

on the front door followed by a hearty 'hello, Fatty,' as Morag led the local doctor into the warm sitting room.

'Oh well, if it isn't Doctor MacLeod,' welcomed Mrs Fletcher. 'Come in, sit down . . . you must be frozen!'

'No, no thank you, I can't wait, you see, I'm in a bit of a hurry.'

'Morag,' said her mother, 'see if your father left anything in the decanter . . . what's the trouble, Neil? They never give you a moment of peace, do they?'

'Well, after all, that's what I'm for,' grinned Neil MacLeod. 'But I've got a bit of a problem . . . you know Peggy na Gròsaid,* the old cailleach that lives away over past Idrigill Point, down by the shore road?'

'Yes, I know her fine; the one that won't let anyone into her house in case they steal her belongings?'

'Yes, and she's accused all the young men in the district of accosting her, too,' put in Morag, 'you'd better watch your step, Doc.'

'Aye, that's just the trouble. You see, Curstag,' (the district nurse) 'is away seeing her sister in Glasgow, and me being a bachelor and fancy free, well, it would be a bit of a risk to call on Peggy. She gave a message to Seadan the Post to come right away. Typical, isn't it now? So, do you think maybe you could . . .'

'Of course, I'll come right away.' And Morag's mother was getting into the old tweed cape that she always kept handy on a hook in the hall, for it was not the first time she had been called on in the district. Indeed, she had very nearly brought as many babies into the world and laid as many corpses as there were days in the year.

Morag had a guilty feeling of relief when they had gone, for

---

* na Gròsaid – the Gooseberry

she loved sometimes to be alone . . . entirely alone, to savour the silence and solitude. She surveyed the room with delight, the arrangement was mostly her own; stark stony backgrounds softened by rich warm colours and fabrics. A fireplace made from stones of the shore housed a flickering wood and peat fire, and in the corner of the room was her father's piano, decked with candles and flowers. 'Get those things off the piano,' he would have said had he been at home, 'you're ruining it.' As if it weren't ruined already! Who could keep a piano on an island as wet as this without it even being tuned . . . mind you, there had been a piano tuner once that visited the islands, but he was a young fellow and had married a local girl. That soon put a stop to his stravaiging about; he's running a discotheque now instead.

Morag moved towards the windows to draw the curtains, then thought better of it – who could close off such a view? Bushes of fuchsia at the end of the garden straggled down to join the tideline on the shore. The sea itself was wild and all lit up. A full moon cast a Jacob's ladder of light straight from the heavens to where she was standing . . . she was, you see, an imaginative girl, would feel suddenly inspired. She thought, or dreamt, felt she saw the men at sea struggling against the fierce pounding of the waves . . . going off course, getting back again . . . cutting down sails . . . clinging to the sides, yelling and choking . . . capsizing, submerging, and somehow she herself was there among it all with her oilskins dripping, gum boots slipping . . . reaching out her hand and gripping a drowning man, her knuckles sore with the cold and strain, his fingernails digging right into her flesh. Suddenly his grip slackened and he drifted away from her view, like a lump of butter melting in a pan of hot black treacle.

She pulled herself together, moved back in the room towards the piano. In a trance she sat and her fingers groped their way onto the keys; gradually the sound of 'Fingal's Cave' left them, scraps of Chopin and now Handel's 'Largo' were filling and overflowing the room. Tears flowed unhindered down her cheeks . . . then faintly over the sound of her playing she thought she heard a tap on the door. Pausing, she listened; it happened again . . . she was alone and afraid, nearly sick with fear. Who could it be? She turned up all the lamps (they still had no electricity, her father hated it so). Then, taking one of them, she braced herself and went to open the door.

It was a young man, tall and handsome, and in no way sinister, though his hair was wet. He seemed to be bleeding from a head wound; the blood was trickling down onto his face.

'What on earth has happened to you?' she said as she helped him in to a better light; his seaman's jersey was soaking and she saw that he was barefoot. 'You'd better come into the kitchen . . . can you manage?' And she seated him down in front of the fire that had been well stacked up in the old-fashioned black kitchen range. 'Take off your jersey! I'll have to bathe that wound myself, as my mother's away with the doctor . . . he'll be bringing her back here, though, so he can attend to it properly then.'

'No,' protested the man, 'I will not need any doctor.'

'Nonsense! Here, drink this! It will do you good,' and she gave him a dram.

Silently he gulped it back, silently he removed his jersey; he seemed reluctant to speak at all. It was not till after she had anxiously treated his wound that he began to relax.

'Can't you tell me what happened?' coaxed Morag. He looked so sad, and there was a strange glitter in his wide black eyes.

Suddenly he smiled at her nearly from ear to ear (for there were few men who could withstand the charms of Morag Fletcher). 'It's my boat . . . I've lost her . . . she's sunk. Maybe you know her, that black fishing ketch that came from over here, belonged to Seannie Menzies?'

'Oh yes, fine I know her; she used to be lying at anchor out there in front of the house. I used to steal aboard her sometimes, pretend I owned her. She was in very bad shape, though!'

'You're telling me! She was the hardest boat I ever tried to handle; I was trying to take her home across the Minch and everything went wrong. The compass was jiggered, the steering went slack . . . everything. I just had to head her round, turn right back with her. Funny thing is, that was what she seemed to be after; everything went fine for a while, till that storm blew up off Idrigill Point and she'd had it. So had I – she dashed herself up against the rocks, there was nothing I could do, the steering had completely gone and you know what the current's like there – vortexes all over the place. There wasn't a hope in hell. I was clinging to the mast when it broke away, and the boom swung at my head, everything went black. Then I suppose I was washed ashore with the rest of the debris.'

'You shouldn't talk of yourself like that. We'll need to let your people know then, won't we . . . Where do you say you come from?'

'I come from beyond the beyond, though I used to come from Stornoway.'

'Gosh, I hope you haven't got concussion . . . is there no one to tell then?'

'No, no one; that's why I came here.'

'Oh, you did right! My mother will do all she can for you. She should be back any minute now. My! Would you look at the time! It's gone nine-thirty . . . could you go a strupag? And I'll make you a sandwich.'

'No, no,' said the man, 'you can give me my jersey back now; it's dry, see for yourself, it's stopped steaming . . .' and quickly, nervously, he pulled it on, started to make for the door. 'It's time for me to go anyway . . . go . . .' his voice faded.

'But you'll need to wait for the doctor . . . and you've nothing on your feet. Wait . . . wait a bit!'

But Morag could not detain him longer; he was out of the front door and down the path without even looking back . . . his tall body seemed to merge into the edge of the moonlight and slowly melt away. There was no sign, no shadow, nothing. So Morag went back into the sitting room, to commune with herself once more. An hour later the doctor's car got back and her mother wearily handed over her cape.

'How was it? What was wrong?' asked Morag.

'A strange case,' answered the doctor. 'It wasn't Peggy at all. It was a young fellow that came banging at her door. Of course she thought he'd come to accost her, till she realised he was half dead. She heaved him into the house and got him onto the bed. She's strong as a horse that one – it's with carrying bags of wet whelks on her back for the best part of half a century.'

'And what happened?' said Morag.

'Well, she shouted to Seadan the Post who happened to be passing the end of her croft, and asked him to fetch me.'

'He died, the poor young fellow,' put in her mother, as she sank wearily into the rocking-chair. 'It was too late. There was nothing either of us could do, the wound on his head had haemorrhaged for far too long.'

'Did he say anything, mother?' asked Morag, the tears flowing from her.

'Not very much, my dear. It's a mystery. As his breath stole slowly away from him he tried to murmur things about a black boat.'

'Washed on the rocks off Idrigill,' continued Morag . . . 'the boom had hit him on the head when the mast broke.'

'Dhia beannaich sinn,'* breathed her mother. 'How did you know that?'

'I know because he was here. He left at half-past nine,' said Morag.

'That's right,' said the doctor, 'that would be just when he died.' Morag buried her head in her mother's lap. There was no consoling her. 'Then it must have been his spirit,' she wept . . . and she wept and wept.

Dhia beannaich sinn – God bless us

Aurora, the Goddess of Dawn

Big Lachie was a fearless and diligent man. He would row out to set his lobster pots each evening and collect them at crack of dawn. No matter what the weather or how heavy the seas, he would go to a favourite spot near Idrigill Point where many a ship had been wrecked, many a sheep had fallen over the steep cliffs to its death. But that didn't stop him from setting his pots there with his own special bait that he would tell no one about – after all, it was hard enough to earn a living without every Tom, Dick or Harry getting in on the act – he a widower with three daughters to keep and feed until they were old enough to wed. That would not be so very long; all three of them were so beautiful it would take your breath away just to look at them.

And that's how he came to choose their names himself, after the loveliest things he could think of – the Aurora-Bore-Alis. The oldest (his favourite) was Aurora, the second Bore, or Babs, and the third Alis (or Alice), his late wife's name. Aurora was already receiving too much attention from a young Norwegian sailor aboard one of the Klondykers (foreign ships tied up alongside Uig pier). He was handsome enough but could hardly speak English, let alone Gaelic, and kept on buying her tins of sweets, since they were far cheaper here than in Norway and he had a sweet tooth himself.

However, the thought of his beautiful daughter being carted away to foreign parts was too much all together fo

Lachie, so when the fine big brochalan of a lad*
came along to ask her hand in marriage, Lachie said, 'No,
she's too young, but if you come back in a year and a day still
in love with her, then she's yours . . . and meanwhile try to
learn the Gaelic.'

So leaving Aurora despondent, the young lover signed on
for South America. And what with jumping ship, gambling,
drink and other diversions, anything to keep his mind off
Aurora, it was considerably more than 'a year and a day'
before he got back. In the meantime the poor girl had worn
herself out scanning the horizon day in and day out. She
didn't eat and couldn't sleep; her father was worried sick
about her. She was even losing her looks in spite of rubbing
her cheeks with beetroot and slapping her face with dockens
to bring back the glow. She even washed her hair in urine to
bring out the highlights as she had seen her grandmother do,
but it was no use – by the time her hero got back she had died
of a broken heart.

Her father vowed that he would never again demand 'a year
and a day'; and this was just as well, for young Bore had grown
into quite a wee smasher meanwhile, and Big Lachie had no
objection whatsoever to her marrying the now prosperous
sailor home from the sea. Anyway, he still had Alis, who was
so like her mother in name and nature and a dab hand at
making bannocks.

And, if you ever find your way across the moor at Idrigill,
look over the steep cliffs lashed by Atlantic breakers, you will
see an outcrop of rock in the form of a woman with a hole in
her head for an eye. She is Idrigill – and if you keep on ,
looking, watching and waiting, she may become 'Aurora, the
Goddess of Dawn' – with a tear in her eye.

* brochalan of a lad – lively young man (cf brochach)

Stem of Infinity

The damp chilly morning was eating into Torquil's bones. He was lazy and sleepy, and depressed. He was still in his bed, lying on the straw mattress on the homemade built-up bed that he and his wife had shared for fifty years. She had been a large woman; he'd teased her often about her weight and her size; the bed wasn't very wide. Sometimes when she was crushing down on him he would say, 'Move over the bed, you great Highland stirk.'

And she would reply, 'Move over yourself, the Cuillin Hills!' because he was tall and thin; his elbows would jab into her from time to time.

However, the poor woman had died a year ago, a year ago today. He had managed well enough without her. He had loved her very dearly in the early days but in recent years she'd been a bit of a menace, coughing and spluttering with the tuberculosis, needing attention every minute of the day and night. And Torquil found himself exhausted. He wasn't a young man, nearing his ninetieth birthday, and he'd wished that he could now follow her to . . . wherever that might be.

Reluctantly, he pulled himself up, stretched and reached with his bare feet for the floor – in this tiny two-room cottage it was made from compressed mud. Many of the cottages in those days were the same; floors rather uneven but with one advantage – they were warm, especially when Torquil had, as he always did, kept the peat fire burning all night long. F knew where he could find his big boots. They would be ur the trust, the elongated wooden settle that reached across in front of the window. So, descending from the bed he struggled over to the trust, put on his thick socks and enormous boots with the criss-cross laces.

He wasn't very sure why he was putting them on or why he had got up, because he didn't have anything to do. He didn't work the croft; had no sheep. He had nothing in fact, very little money. Just a few shillings stowed in a hole in the wall where he and his wife had kept the Bible and her false teeth. He himself had still got a couple of stumps left, just enough to eat aran-coirce, or oatcake, which he chewed; and he gave himself a bowl of milk. He couldn't be bothered making himself brose or porridge, in fact he couldn't be bothered doing anything at all. He had a sore back, a headache and the rheumatics were killing him . . . killing him. This made him think about the burial of his wife.

Just a year ago; seemed like a long time now since she had died. He'd had some help from the villagers, the minister and some relations on the mainland to get her buried, and what a stramash that had been. The trouble was that Torquil's plot in the graveyard on this island was already full. His ancestors went back for centuries, they'd been buried one on top of another for years and years. He remembered well the rainy, miserable, midgie day on which Christina his wife had been buried.

The men all had their half cut, their bottle of whisky with them of course, in their back pockets; who would be without it? And they took their spades, dug into the grave to make space for Christina's enormous bulk. She'd had to have a large coffin, it was a problem to know what to do. They thought they might have to build a mound and get her in that way; when they opened up the ground, the first ones they came across were the bones of Finlay, his uncle. He was on top of

Murdo Gillies, and God knows who the bones belonged to beneath that. But, as I said, they went on for centuries. His cousin Dougie MacRae from the mainland had suggested that they take her for burial over there.

'Oh,' said Torquil, 'no indeed! I would rather see her dead first.' He'd forgotten in his confused mind, but then realised, of course, that she was dead. Poor Torquil. He would now have to look after himself and he didn't know for how long. But he was pretty sure he would be following her by the end of the winter. Although the doctor had seen him, he knew by the way he'd said, 'Oh, you'll be all right, Torquil, just you take it easy,' he knew quite well in himself that he had not much time to go. So, what to do? 'Well, first of all,' he thought to himself as he kicked the hens out through the main door of his cottage, 'why not do as my ancestors did? I'll take a slice of oatcake and a bannock or two, tie them in my handkerchief and with my cromag on my shoulder walk and walk till I drop.'

So, dousing the peat fire by generously, liberally pissing on it, he fetched the key of his house, and, removing the corn dolly from above the lintel, his good luck token which he put in his pocket, he strolled forth bravely. Down the croft he went, the wild flowers growing in abundance, as the croft had not been cultivated for a good many years now. There was everything on it that shouldn't be on it, like gorse and thistles, kingcups and buttercups, clover galore. And here and there the nests of birds – the corncrake, for instance had been their regular visitor, driving him potty at night, cnoc-cnoc-cnocing – but now he would be leaving it all behind.

At the end of the croft were seven magnificent, ancient beech trees. Like himself they were gnarled and pitted, twisted as though they too were suffering from osteo-arthritis. He loved them all. They were in fact his friends; he talked to them regularly. Now one by one he said his au revoirs. He f like hugging them, their great wide twisted trunks; he felt emotional, as though he would like to embrace each one separately. Because he knew in his heart he would never see them again.

He thought he would do his walking in stages. So he took the high road up by Luib, and crossed country, absorbed all the magnificent views: in the distance he could see the Quiraing and on a beautiful day he would have been able to see the small islands, Pabay, Raasay, Scalpay and Guillamon glittering in the sun, as it used to be in his young days. He walked some ten miles or so and then, like his ancestors before him, he stopped. He must eat some of his oatcake.

So, he settled down beside a stream, watching the brown foam gurgling on its surface. Then undoing his spotted handkerchief he extracted a piece of bannock and was just about to devour it when a voice in his ear said, 'Greedy, greedy, fàg e – leave it, leave it!' He thought it must be a gull, so he threw a bit for the seagulls. But then he realised there were no birds. So whose was the voice? He didn't eat any more. Tucking it back in his handkerchief and tying it to his cromag, he got up and proceeded to walk further on.

He was weary already by the time he'd passed Sligachan, and had yet to climb up the mountainside of Druim nan Cleochd.* It was a steep, rugged road, and he was astonished to find a hearse coming towards him driven by James the Undertaker whom he knew well.

'Ca'eil thu 'dol?' (Where are you going?)

'A'n Ath Leathan,' said the undertaker. (I'm going to Broadford.)

'Oh well,' said Torquil, 'I've just left there.'

'Where for?' said James.

Druim nan Cleochd – Back (ridge) of the Cloak

'God knows!' said Torquil.

'Oh well, you look worn out already,' James said. 'You could do with a wee dram.' He proceeded to undo the hearse and lift from the coffin a bottle of Bullochlade and a sandwich. 'Gabh e,' (take a swig of that) he said in Gaelic and offered him a sandwich.

Well, Torquil was a mannerly man and always very sociable. He didn't like to say 'no' and indeed he needed the sandwich and particularly the wee dram. Then saying 'cheerio' to the undertaker they went their ways – Torquil climbing up to the top of the hill, then down again towards Sconser. He didn't dilly-dally there but proceeded to walk – his strength leaving him and becoming more and more exhausted with every step. He would try to make it to Penifiler* and the head of the loch. Because not far from that was the graveyard: if he could get there it would be a good place to stop for good and all.

By the time he got to the graveyard night had fallen, so he just snuggled down behind a gravestone elaborately carved with a beautiful angel. He was now beginning to hallucinate; felt he saw the angel take off from its stone and soar up into the night sky fluttering its beautiful white wings. He then said a prayer he had learned at his mother's knee:

> This night as I lay down to sleep
> I pray the Lord my soul to keep;
> If I should die before I wake
> I pray the Lord my soul to take.

This had always frightened him a bit. When he was young and happy, little and playful, he didn't really want to die. But now

* Penifiler – Peighinn nam fidhlear (Pennyland of the fiddlers)

of course it was a different story. Gradually he fell asleep and perhaps it was because of the prayer, perhaps because of the angel, but somehow or other he seemed to get a second wind, an increase of strength, even of vigour.

So as morning dawned he stretched himself, relieved himself and, although he wouldn't eat, he decided to proceed on from Penifiler to Cuidrach, that lovely haunted bay he remembered so well from the days when he would walk to Uig with a bull to be taken to the cow. He was getting very weak now, his breath was going from him. He would have to stop every now and then, he had a long way to go yet before he would reach whatever his destination might be – perhaps it would be Kensaleyre. He would try for that anyway.

So he strode on bravely. But by the time he reached Kensaleyre he was physically spent – his knees were going, his mind was going, he was faint, weak and shaky – without knowing what was happening, he collapsed.

It so happens he collapsed at the gates of a very large house. A wee bandy-legged man came trotting down the path. It so happened he was the lay minister, temporarily staying there, he'd prepared laboriously what he thought to be a very fine sermon. A really fine sermon which he intended to deliver in the ancient church down the road, where the notorious Maighstir Ruairidh used to preach. He was so excited – by the time he got to the gate he hadn't noticed Torquil lying there, and stepped across him. In his haste he wondered if he'd soiled the end of his trouser leg, or his shoe in doing this, so he whipped out his immaculate handkerchief and re-polished his shoes. Then proceeded, without even taking a look at Torquil. He was in such a hurry to convert some more unwilling sinners.

Meanwhile the spirit had departed from poor Torquil and was now heading for heaven knows where. But the strange thing is, up at the big house when the chamber-maid was carrying a hot water bottle and a glass with senna pods up the stairs for the minister's return – she was stopped in her tracks. It was a huge staircase that branched off to the left and to the right; at the top of it in the centre was an enormous window. The trees were silhouetted outside it and a full moon was streaming in, lighting the whole place up. Against this light was the distinct shadow of a man, a ghost.

'A Thighearna!* gasped the maid, dropping the hot water bottle. She nearly collapsed in a dead faint. And people do say that to this very day you can see a form of a man up on the top of the staircase. They consider it's a punishment for the minister who had neglected to attend to the stranded corpse of Torquil.

It was not more than ten days later that James found himself on the road again, this time making a return journey with the hearse up the steep hill that led to the top of Druim na' Cleochd, where he stood for a while to think about and remember his friend, and of course to toast his health. So once again, he raised the coffin lid, found his half bottle and sandwich and put up a toast – this time to Torquil:

> A h-uile latha
> A chi's nach fhaic
> (Every day
> Whether I see you or not, my friend.)

And then he turned to enjoy the view as he sipped his dram. He was looking right across to the wonderful sixty-foot waterfall – the straight white fall the children call 'Granny's Hair' – that flows down through a cleft in the mountains from the top of Druim nan Cleochd (the back or the width of a

---

* A Thighearna! – Oh, good Lord!

cape). It is the cape that sometimes hides the Cuillin Hills, and sometimes reveals them in all their glory.

And it seemed to him as though an angel had dropped its white wing down upon the waterfall . . . or was it just the waterfall itself? Or, was it the angel that Torquil had talked to, prayed to back at the Penifiler graveyard? Nobody will ever know the answers. So James just finished his dram and proceeded on with the remains of poor Torquil, taking him back home to his cottage and his trees for burial.

It was customary in those days in country places like Wales and the Highlands to walk till you dropped. And likewise, in the Arctic, they had the habit of putting the old ones out in the snow – to sit till they froze to death.

Guide to Pronunciation

Vowels	English sound equivalent	Gaelic examples
a	short like *a* in *cat*	na, amadan
à	long like *a* in *far*	blà, slàinte
e	short like *e* in *get*	e, uisge
i	short like *i* in *king*; or *e* in *me*	sin; nighean, Iain
ì	long like *ee* in *feet*	crìoch
o	short like *o* in *modest*	mo, ort, bochan,
ò	long like *a* in *awe*	Gròsaid
ó	long like *o* in *bold*	mór
u	long like *oo* in *poor*	Curstag, Cuil

Consonants

b	at beginning of word like *b* in *boat*; elsewhere like *p* in *captive*	Beinn, ban-sìth; chlab
bh	at beginning and end like *v*, but can be silent at end	Bhàn, falabh, obh; dubh, badaibh-bàth
c	at beginning like *c* in *can*; in middle or at end like *chk*	cailleach; Mhic
ch	as *ch* in *loch* (never *ch* in *cheer*)	Cheò, bochan, quaich
chd	like *ch* with *k* added	Cleochd, beannachd
d	at beginning like *d* in *drew*; elsewhere like *t* in *cattle*; before e or *i* like *j* in *jet*	duin, Duntulm; Seadan, Sad, udalain; dearbh, cnàide
dh	guttural like *ch* but less explosive before or after *a*, *o*; before or after *e*, *i* like *y* in *yield*; in middle and at end of word silent	dhuit, dhuibh; Dhia; oidhche, céilidh, a'gheallaidh
f	as in English	Farquhar, falaisgair

fh	at beginning of word silent	fheamainn
g	at beginning or before *a, o, u* like *g* in *go*; elsewhere like *ck* in *neck*	glaoich, Gagach, sgapadh; stapag, Mallaig, uisge, sgian
gh	before or after *i, e* like y in *yield*; in middle and at end of words silent as in *night*	ghealach, gheallaidh; àigh, nighean
l	similar to *l* in *lure*; darker next to *a, o, u*	Cuil, leibh, leat; falabh, Scalpay
ll	flanked by *i* and *e* like *ll* in *million*; otherwise like *ll* in *pull*	cailleach; Mallaig, Caillich steall
m	like *m* in English	mise, nam, amadan
mh	at beginning and end like *v* in English; in middle generally silent	Mhic, mhór; sàmhach
n	similar to English; before *e, i* like *n* in *not*; after *c, g, m, t* usually like *r*	an, na; sin, nighean; cnoc, cnàide
nn	flanked by *a, o, u* like *ion* in *onion*; after *i* like *n* in *pinion*	beannaich; puinneag
p	like *p* in English	Pabay, strupag
r	like English, with more of a roll	crùisgean, Máiri, Raasay, mór
rt	as *rst* or *rsht*	ort, ceart
s	before or after *a, o, u* like English *ss*; before or after *e, i*, like *sh*	Sad, Raasay, iasg, suas; sinn buidseach, Seòras, Aiseag
t	before or after *a, o, u* like *t* in *tone*; before or after *e, i*, like *ch* in *chin*	Curstag, Duntulm; slàinte
th	at beginning often like *h* in *hat*, but can be silent; in middle and at end silent	tha, Sgitheanach, Beathag; bàth

Combinations of *lb, lp, lm*, interpolate a drawl vowel between them

falbh, Duntulm

Guide to Pronunciation

Dipthongs

ai	like *a* in *that* if first syllable, otherwise short like *i* in *thin*; at end of word before *d*, like *itch*	caileag, Iain, beannaich; A'Gheallaidh; Ealasaid
ài	long like *a* in *father*	Màiri, slàinte
ao	between English *oo* and *ee*	ghaol
ea	like *e* in *red*; or can be like *ya* in yacht	Beathag, nighean; Ealasaid, seallaibh, puinneag
éi	like *a* in *fate*	céilidh, éirigh
ei	like *i* in *thin*	Beinn, leibh, Eilean
eò	*e* slightly sounded and *o* like *a* in *yawn*	Seòras, Cheò
ia, ìo	*ee-a* as in *me-and-you*	Dia, iasg, crìoch, fior
oi	as *a* in *awe*	oidhche
ui	*u* like *oo* in *poor*, *i* silent	Quiraing, uisge, puinneag

Tripthong

aoi	sound of the dipthong *ao* with *i* silent; as French 'eui'	glaoich, ghaoil

Glossary

amadan	– fool, rascal
an	– the
Annag	– young Anne
aran-coirce	– oatcake
argy-bargy	– haggling
aslaig	– aslaich, a breast
badaibh-bàth	– pas de bas, Irish jig
ban-sìth	– female fairy who wails before death or disaster
Balmoral	– kind of bonnet worn to one side
Beathag	– Rebecca
bairns	– children
bealach	– pass of a mountain, glen
Beinn na Caillich	– 'peak of the old woman'; name of individual mountains above Broadford and Kylerhea
big	– old; great
Blà Bheinn	– the warm mountain (by Torrin)
blethering	– talking nonsense
bochan	– cottage, hut, bower
bodach	– old or churlish man
Book, The	– The *Holy Bible*
boormaister	– coarse laird, nasty man
buidseach	– a spell
Bulloch lade	– local island whisky
caileag	– girl
cailleach	– single woman, old woman
Cairistiona	– Christina
caman	– shinty stick
céilidh	– party, visit for entertainment and news
cladach	– shore
creatuir	– creature
cromag	– crook
crowdie	– oatmeal and water uncooked

crùbach	– ignoble, mean, shrivelling
crùisgean	– oil-lamp
Cuillins	– mountains of Minginish, south Skye
Curstag	– Kirsty
each	– horse
gaol	– beloved object or person
glaoich	– fool
grape	– iron-pronged fork used in farming
half-spiffed	– tipsy
heid	– head
keis(h)t	– ciste-chaol, wooden settee with bottom and sides closed in and lid on top, about seven feet long
ken	– comprehension
kingcups	– big yellow flowers growing in ditches
machair	– grasslands above shoreline
midgie	– midge-ridden
Minch, the	– very unpredictable ocean passage between Skye and the Outer Hebrides
Mod, the	– annual Gaelic festival of music and story
mór	– old; great
Nick, old	– the Devil
niste	– now
n-òt	– sterling pound note
oot	– out
pibroch	– ceòl mór, classical Highland bagpipe music
Post, the	– Post Office postman
puinneag	– common sorrel
put up	– vomited
quaichs	– shallow bowl-shaped drinking cups
Quiraing	– 'the round fold', Jurassic age rock labyrinths and landslide of north Skye
rudha	– promontory
Sassenach	– Englishman
Seadan	– name of local postman
Seannie	– Johnnie
Seumas	– James
spout-fish	– razor fish, a common mollusc
sgùrr	– sharp-pointed hill
sìthean	– fairies
stapag	– mixture of oatmeal and cream
stirk	– bullock

Glossary

Strath	– district of south Skye including Broadford, valley of Strath behind it, Strathaird and Corry; MacKinnon country
stravaiging	– wandering
strupag	– cup of tea
Talya	– name for a'ghealach, the moon
targer	– violent, domineering person
Timbuktu	– back of beyond
trust	– truis-àite, blanket chest
uisge	– water
uist	– wheesht, silence!
WRI	– Women's Rural Institute

POLYGON is an imprint of Birlinn Limited. Our list includes titles by Alexander McCall Smith, Liz Lochhead, Kenneth White, Robin Jenkins and other critically acclaimed authors. Should you wish to be put on our catalogue mailing list **contact**:

Catalogue Request
Polygon
West Newington House
10 Newington Road
Edinburgh EH9 1QS
Scotland, UK

Tel: +44 (0) 131 668 4371
Fax: +44 (0) 131 668 4466
e-mail: info@birlinn.co.uk

Postage and packing is free within the UK. For overseas orders, postage and packing (airmail) will be charged at 30% of the total order value.

Our complete list can be viewed on our website. Go to **www.birlinn.co.uk** and click on the Polygon logo at the top of the home page.